THEY CALL US MONSTERS

An Omnibus

BRIAN KNIGHT

Tulpa Books

____

ALSO BY BRIAN KNIGHT

____

Horror - Novels

- Feral
- Broken Angel
- Hacks

Horror - Omnibus

- They Call Us Monsters

Horror - Chapbooks

- Children of Filth
- Heart of the Monster
- Apocalypse Green
- Johnny Junk
- Death is Blind
- Midnight Blues
- The Beast Inside - The Berserkers, Part 1
- Blood Rage - The Berserkers, Part 2

Horror - Collections

- Dragonfly

The Phoenix Girls - Fantasy

- The Conjuring Glass (Book 1)
- The Crimson Brand (Book 2)
- The Heart of the Phoenix (Book 3)

The Misadventures of Butch Quick - Crime

- A Face Full of Ugly - A Chapbook
- Big Trouble in Little Boots - A Chapbook
- Sex, Death, and Honey (Book 1)

*For Lisa Lee Tone, who knows that homonyms are not my
friends.*

ACKNOWLEDGMENTS

I read once that no book is written alone. I can't remember who said it, otherwise I would attribute it properly, but it is the sentiment, not the source, that matters here.

I would like to take a moment to thank the folks who were involved with these stories over the years. Feel free to skip ahead a few pages if this kind of shit bores you, no one will mind, but I need to give these fine people their due.

Chris Hedges, D'Ann Hedges, and Paul Danda of Insidious Publications were a joy to work with, and Chris's hand built, hand stitched hardcovers were and are true works of art. My hardcover contributor copy 1200 AM Live is one of the most prized books in my collection.

Tom Moran and Billie Moran, owners of both Sideshow Press and Gallows Press, provided me with some of my best publishing experiences. Tom also provided the fantastic artwork for the first editions on The Avian and They Call Us Monsters.

Special thanks are due to Tom Moran and Hannah Walthers, the artist who provided several fine pieces for the original edition of 1200 AM Live. Both have kindly agreed to let me use their original cover art for the stories collected in this omnibus, and Hannah allowed me to use some of her previously unused art for the cover and interior of this new edition.

Both Hannah and Tom are gifted genre artists, and wonderful people. I don't deserve friends like them, but I'm sure happy to have them.

Last, but certainly not least, thanks to my first readers and editors, Lisa Lee Tone and H Michael Casper. I don't know what I'd do without their generosity.

Brian Knight

1200 AM LIVE!

Part 1 of the They Call Us Monsters Omnibus

1200
3amLIVE
Brian Knight

CHAPTER 1

10:00 PM

Joe Carter tuned the radio to his favorite station, cursing the dayshift driver's love of shit-kicker music. They played the shit endlessly at the office. He had to suffer through it whenever he was on hold with dispatch.

"This is Coast to Coast AM, and tonight we're discussing alien abduction with special guest ..."

He turned the volume down and radioed dispatch.

"This is Carter, driver 008, taking vehicle 1011 out on the Railroad Avenue route."

He grimaced through several seconds of the musical stylings of Toby Keith coming from the two way radio before dispatch acknowledged. The fact that he could now recognize several individual shit-kicker singers dismayed him.

He turned the radio back up and drove his patrol car, an unimpressive little Geo Metro, out of Bailey Security's auto yard and joined the sparse Friday evening traffic headed toward what promised to be another uneventful night.

Except for the few wandering crazies who favored the scuzzy industrial district, one in particular whose almost nightly sermons were absolute miracles of vulgarity, Lewiston's nightlife was a bit on the tame side. There were the occasional crackheads, runaways, and bums, but overall, they just weren't very interesting.

Not like Boise at all. Boise was a real city, just as he had been a real cop until the goat-screw at The Doll House.

Within five minutes, during which the late evening traffic seemed almost to vanish, Joe found himself in what he thought of as The Derelict District. He turned down a short access road beside an equipment rental center and then left onto Railroad Avenue.

Railroad Avenue, an *Authorized Vehicles Only* back-street, started near the center of town and branched off the levee bypass road. Its gated entrance was obscured by a growth of willows that fronted the bypass parkway and ran about a mile between the railroad tracks and Snake River levy, ending east of town at the gate of the pulp mill.

The mill was his biggest fish on the route, and Rail-road Avenue's primary traffic, trucks running to and from the mill, vanished after 5 pm.

Joe's only scenery along that stretch of paved boredom were the ass ends of a car dealership, the rental center, a pawnshop, a cell tower, and two propane storage tanks the size of semitrucks. Between the bridge underpass and the mill, there was the 24th Street exit, a yard of criss-crossed tracks and idle railcars, and a whole lot of nothing.

Railroad Avenue's infrequent foot traffic came from three directions. There were walkers from the levee bypass parkway who usually made it no farther than the cell tower before realizing they had left the park behind. There were vagrants who descended the footpath from the bridge. The worst were the druggies and crazies who filtered down from 24th Street.

24th Street was a narrow, crumbling road that jabbed through Lewiston's nastiest residential area – Crack Town - like a scabbed finger. It started about midway on Railroad Avenue and ended at the point of a high-peaked hill that overlooked downtown Lewiston.

Joe had driven the full length of Railroad Avenue twice before anything interesting happened.

CHAPTER 2

11:00 PM

Joe caught the girl in his spotlight under the bridge over-pass, her skirt hiked up to her naked hips. One hand worked frantically at the junction of her thighs while she spray-painted the concrete abutment.

"Mother fucker," he said, bringing the Metro to a full stop and watching the girl, who seemed oblivious to her new audience. Maybe she'd seen him and just didn't care.

Without a doubt one of the crazies from Crack Town, stoned out of her fucking mind he imagined, but a damn fine specimen all the same. Slender, a wild tangle of blonde hair falling over her shoulders and back, perky wineglass tits pressing out the front of a t-shirt so short and tight it could have been a sports bra. Her bare, flat belly gleamed with the sweat of her efforts.

She could have been a well-developed fourteen years old or a very petite twenty-four, it was impossible to tell from the distance between them. For Joe, the ambiguity made her more exciting.

She was moaning, very loudly, something that might have been *fucky – fucky - fucky*.

The easy thing to do, the thing he would normally do if the vandal was not marking a client's property, would be to give his horn a honk and scare her away. What he was supposed to do was radio dispatch and have them call the police while he sat tight.

Joe did neither of these things.

Turning Coast to Coast AM off, he put the Metro in park and got out slowly, trying not to startle her.

The girl still did not notice, or care. Her left hand worked quicker than ever below the bunched-up skirt and the spray paint flew in circles, loops, and sharp angles over the concrete abutment of the underpass. When he'd crept to within ten feet of where she stood, he could make out her frenzied words.

"Sucky, fucky, doggie-style, do-dah, do-dah …"

He paused in his steps, shocked, and a little impressed by the simplistic vulgarity of her rhyme.

He could also make out her face and age better.

Bug-eyed stoned, but otherwise a real stunner. Well-shaped, a sexy rasp of voice, the angular but soft face of a mischievous pixie. She had striking eyes of a strange, deep honey color.

As for her age, he thought it was closer to the bottom end of his original estimation, fifteen or sixteen, maybe, but no older than nineteen.

With one last curlicue flourish, she tossed her spray-paint aside and doubled her efforts below her waist, both hands now working in furious circles.

Joe moved closer.

"Sucky, fucky, doggie-style …," she sang.

Painted on the concrete before her was a parade of stick figures in various poses, from the erotic to the violent. One held what appeared to be a sword in one hand and a severed head in the other. Another bent forward, giving itself a blowjob. One had what he thought were bird's wings for arms, and a narrow beaked bird's head.

Written below these in large, runny letters was the legend *1200 AM Live Makes Me Wet!*, and *The Bird Man Has A Big Pecker!*

Joe had to bite his lip to keep from bursting into laughter as he closed the distance to her. She was still unaware of his presence, still fully focused on her own business. He grabbed her arms, pulling them quickly behind her back and locking them tightly in one of his large fists before she could even think to struggle.

"Bad girl," he said, keeping her faced away from him as he glanced around. There was no one in sight, not even the sound of traffic on the bridge above. The night was his. "You know it's not nice to deface public property."

She giggled, a conspiratorial sound, as if they were sharing some kind of joke, and turned her head to look at him.

He gripped her hair with his free hand and forced her to face forward again.

"Nope," he said, endeavoring to sound kindly and helpful. "Best face forward now. Don't want to run into anything and mark up your pretty head."

He urged her forward, around the abutment, into the deep shadows cast by the bridge.

"We need to get you home now," he said. "Don't want you getting into any more trouble."

She nodded, still giggling, and let him steer her without protest, as though the backside of the abutment he'd caught her defacing was indeed her home.

"Okay now, I need to check you for weapons before I let you go," he said, releasing her hands.

They immediately sought the refuge of her crotch again, and Joe felt the fat dangle of his prick stiffen and press against the inside of his uniform pants.

"No, we'll take care of that soon enough. You need to lean forward and put your hands against the wall."

She did without a pause and began singing her dirty little rhyme again.

"Now spread your legs a little so I can pat you down."

She did, and a shift of the breeze brought her scent, previously overpowered by the stink of Railroad Avenue, to his flaring nostrils.

Joe pushed her skirt over the curve of her ass with his left hand, now bug-eyed himself with pure excitement, and unbuckled his belt with the other.

Life was tough, but sometimes it still threw Joe Carter a bone.

Later, as he cruised again, returning from the mill end of Railroad Avenue, he saw the girl stumbling back up the broken little road toward Crack Town. She did not pause at his approach or look back over her shoulder at him. She had quit the singing and laughing though. She seemed to be coming down from whatever high she was on.

He wondered, not for the first time since leaving her ass up in the darkness behind the bridge abutment, if he shouldn't have smothered her and tossed her in the river.

He pushed the thought aside quickly as she disappeared past the rise at the end of a short, sharp incline.

She would most likely never remember their night's fun by the river, or if she did, only bits and pieces, like a few scattered pieces of some surrealistic puzzle. Even if she remembered everything, she hadn't seen his face.

Joe supposed he was safe enough.

He passed the abutment once more and prepped his flashlight to search the premises around the fenced-in propane storage tanks, and a tank car parked next to it.

He saw his young crack bunny's message, spray painted a bright and dripping red on the concrete.

1200 AM Live Makes Me Wet!

He'd driven in silence since leaving the girl. He turned the radio back on, but after the night's excitement, all of the blues, grays, and tentacled monsters who may have been flying their saucers around this great rock, landing every now and then to carve up a cow or probe some poor country rube, seemed a dull subject.

He turned the dial to 1200, knowing there was nothing but static on that frequency, he knew the AM dial back to front, but desperate for something more exciting than conspiracy theories and Sci-Fi geek fantasies.

He was still a little disappointed when he turned out to be right. Weak and uninteresting static.

At that hour of the night, the only thing on the AM dial was recycled news, bible thumpers, and a few holdovers from the old days when music still dominated the AM dial, all country music. Or, of course, the aliens.

He turned the volume dial down all the way, opting for some silence in which to replay his unexpected encounter of the night a few more times in his mind.

CHAPTER 3

12:00 AM

Joe pulled over at a wide spot in the road and bent sideways to reach for his logbook. After updating his log, it wuld be time to call dispatch with his *Twelve O'clock and All's Well*. He nearly jumped out of his skin when the radio's speakers gave a high-pitched squeal, like feedback.

"Holy Hell!" He snatched up the logbook, gave the radio's glowing display a filthy look, and twisted the volume dial with his free hand.

He was reaching for the tuner dial when he registered that the static was gone, replaced by a flat, but expectant, silence. He froze, confused, then his eyes caught the time display. 11:59 glowed a fuzzy green, blinked, and became 12:00.

Joe smiled as the sound of an electric guitar broke the silence, a slow and grinding heavy metal riff followed by pounding bass and the orgasmic groaning of a woman.

Bumper music.

1200 AM was not just the frequency, it seemed.

Though the production sounded high quality, Joe thought it must be a ham radio broadcast. Somehow, Joe supposed, the broadcaster had managed to pirate the unused frequency. He didn't think it was legal for ham operators to broadcast on public frequencies.

The disc jockey's first line of banter cemented his suspicion to a certainty.

"Good morning to all you sick bastards out there. I'm Andy Crow with the Dirty Crow radio network, and this is 1200 AM Live, live at 12:00 AM!" The man's voice was high and sharp, like no DJ Joe had ever heard, but he spoke his lines like a seasoned pro. "Here's a great big Dirty Crow welcome for all you newbies, a big thanks to Little Lisa Ray for helping to spread the word, and a big suck my dick to all the scuttling little roaches at the FCC. Catch me if you can, motherfuckers!"

Joe was surprised into laughter, but also a little shocked. Vulgarity was nothing new to him, and it had never particularly bothered him, but he was not used to hearing such language over public airwaves.

A second, slightly deeper voice joined in as the bumper music faded.

"Holy Mary Mother of fuck! Charles Greene here, making radio history while you sit around with your peckers in your hands."

Joe laughed harder as a comic jumble of slapstick sound effects filled the cab of his patrol car —*arooogahs* and *boy-oy-oings*, the skid and bang of a crashing car, a prodding sound, followed by an *oooff!* straight from the Three Stooges archives.

"What time is it?" Andy Crow shouted.

Charles Greene responded, his voice strained and rough. "Half past a monkey's ass, a quarter to his balls?"

The grating blat of a game show buzzer sounded.

"Wrong," Crow said.

"So what fucking time *is* it?" Greene again.

As if on cue, which Joe supposed it was, a chorus of voices called out "It's time for *What's That Sound!*"

Ding-ding-ding-ding!

"Yes, it's time for the old 1200 AM Live favorite, *What's That Sound*, where the members of our captive audience take turns guessing at the mystery sound. The winner gets Dirty Crow radio's spotlight treatment and will make their confession in the first hour of the show, before the listening audience starts to lose their heads."

Joe had been so focused on the program that he'd remained parked at the side of Railroad Avenue.

"Dispatch to Carter. You there, Joe?" Bailey Security's dispatch startled him out of his grinning daze.

"Pestering bitch," he said, turning the volume knob down and picking up his two-way. Then, straining for a polite tone, "Sorry, got sidetracked."

"That's fine," she said. "Anything new happen?"

"Naw," Joe said, anxious to be finished with the conversation so he could turn this interesting new show back up. "Some graffiti on the underpass, but I didn't see who did it. That's all."

No immediate response from her end, so Joe tossed his two-way onto the passenger seat and cranked the volume before opening the logbook.

Crow and Greene's vulgar banter had ceased, and there was a slobbering, sloppy sound coming from the radio.

Joe's jaw dropped.

"There it is, folks! The 1200 AM Live Mystery Sound."

Sounds like fucking, Joe thought, and his amusement returned. *Now this is what radio should be like!*

"That's finger banging," a man from the *captive audience* volunteered.

The buzzer blatted again.

"Close, but no dice," Crow shouted. "Next."

"Was it a queef?" someone else asked.

"You stupid bastard," Crow said, sounding genuinely angry. "Last night's sound was a queef."

"Security," Greene shouted. "Get that stupid mother-fucker outa' here."

Shouted protests in the background, some kind of minor scuffle that had to have been more canned audio effects, like the mystery sound itself.

"Listen, folks," Crow cut in, sounding supremely annoyed, "this is a pretty much anything goes show, but there are two simple things you need to remember if you want to be a guest. Only two!" He shouted the last word, startling Joe.

Dirty Crow's got a temper, Joe thought, scribbling his initials in the log and flipping it closed. *If it's an act, it's a good one.*

"No call-ins," Greene said in a deadpan tone. "We don't give out our number, so don't go fucking looking for it. You want on the air, you have to find us."

"And for fuck's sake," Crow cut in, "pay attention! That's all we ask!"

Nope, not an act. All good humor had dropped from Crow's voice. The hard edge in his voice was true rage.

Joe checked Railroad Avenue to make sure it was clear

before pulling out and drove. He checked the road to Crack Town in his rear-view. Still deserted.

"Blowjob," a woman from the audience volunteered. "Sounds like a blowjob to me."

Ding-ding-ding-ding!

"*And we have a winner,*" Crow shouted.

"Not surprised in the least, if I may say so," Greene offered. "You strike me as a woman familiar with that sound."

"That *is* in fact the sound of Mr. Greene having his cock gobbled as we speak. Again, thanks to Little Lisa Ray for her help."

"Fuckin' A," Greene volunteered. "Lisa is the best intern ever!"

There were more of the slobbery, sucking sounds, then a wet smack and a giggling voice that made Joe jump in alarm.

"It's all about dedication," Lisa said, and to Joe she sounded just like the girl he'd had by the bridge underpass. She giggled again and went back to her intern's duties with an enthusiastic slurping sound.

A guilty panic froze Joe's mind for a moment, and he was certain that God, or karma, had placed that little crackhead in the studio to rat him out, to punish him for fucking up the second chance he'd been given. Then Joe passed the bridge abutment again, saw the message spray-painted there, and the panic hand twisting his stomach loosened. He relaxed with the realization that karma, God, or coincidence had nothing to do with that girl being in 1200 AM Live's studio, and with the certainty that if she was going to rat him out, she would have done it at once.

Well, maybe not a certainty, but a probability. Most likely, she didn't even remember, and even if she did, she hadn't seen his face or even his car as far as he knew.

I was stupid, he thought. *I was careless*. Joe didn't regret what he'd done to her, not even for a moment, only that he'd been careless enough to let her walk away.

He did his best to put her out of his mind as he drove down Railroad Avenue, and 1200 AM Live continued.

The residue of Joe's fear melted away quickly as the show continued, and he got a sense of what the show was about. 1200 AM Live, Dirty Crow Radio, was a pornographic crossing of the creative vulgarity of Howard Stern or Don and Mike, and the Advice Shows with hosts who may or may not have the credentials they claimed, shows that were more dirty laundry confessionals than advice.

Except there were no call-ins, which made sense since Misters Crow and Greene were probably breaking more laws than even they knew. He wondered where they broadcasted from, and decided their studio was likely mobile. He didn't know how, but he imagined the Feds had ways of tracking down airwave pirates.

The woman who had won *What's That Sound* told her story, made her confession, with many interruptions by the hosts, who never outright mocked her, but often flirted on the edges of mockery. It was a great yet pathetic story of sex addiction. The woman had sex with everyone. She had sex with her husband's friends, with her co-workers, with men she met over the internet, with strangers she met walking in the park.

Though entertaining, it was stuff he'd heard before on the Shock Jock shows he could tune into in bigger and better cities. It wasn't until after the interview that it got really interesting.

"Sometimes I really wish this was a picture show," Crow said with a raucous titter. "Mr. Greene is on what you might call a fact checking mission."

"Yes indeed! So many shows these days neglect to do the necessary research, but we here at 1200 AM Live – Dirty Crow Radio, we take our calling seriously."

"The subject has now stripped and assumed the position. Tell us Mr. Greene, what's her clam like?"

"Not bad," Greene said. "Clean shaven, a pleasing shade of pink. Plenty of mileage but still in good condition."

"So, what's the verdict?" Crow asked.

"Well used, but not abused." Greene said.

"So, we know she can use it, but I'm still not entirely convinced. The big question is how well she can use it. Get the mic down there."

"Well fuck me," Joe said in pure amazement at the sound of a zipper. The zipper sound was followed by a grunt and groan of mingled pleasure and pain, then a series of wet slaps, and the occasional loud *whack* as Greene slapped her ass.

"Move it around! Don't just lay there. Work with me!"

"Now that is what I call job satisfaction," Crow commented.

"If you can't enjoy your work," Greene said, now puffing with exertion, "you might as well give it up."

The wet slap-slap-slap grew in tempo, and the woman's steady grunts and moans became wheezy little screams.

"I think Mr. Greene is about to dump his junk," Crow commented. "Either that, or he's put on a Goofy mask."

Driving his route on Railroad Avenue, but no longer paying the slightest attention to anything but the radio, Joe barked laughter.

With a last loud smack of sweaty genitals, Greene roared his pleasure. "Fuck yeah!"

The woman shrieked, a sound that might have indicated extreme pleasure, mortal agony, or both at once.

Then she was silent.

After a few moments, Greene spoke again.

"Well, honestly she was a bit of a dead fuck, but even a dead fuck is better than no fuck at all."

CHAPTER 4

1:00 AM

Joe pulled over next to the underpass abutment and unzipped facing the graffiti. For a moment he didn't think he'd b able to pass water through the hard-on that jutted over his shorts, but finally it did flow in uneven spurts.

He'd been a talk radio fan for many years, but this was the first time a show had given him a boner.

When he stepped back to the car, he heard Crow's voice again, reading a bizarre parody of the local news.

"...Welcome our special guest newswoman, on loan from The King of All Media himself, Miss Black Howard Stern – Charlie Superfly!"

There's a Miss Black Howard Stern now? I've missed a lot since he went to satellite, Joe thought.

"Wuzup bitches!" Charlie Superfly sang a few lines to her intro music, a short rhythm and blues number.

"You are one sexy sista," Greene commented.

Charlie giggled.

"You know it, baby! In local news today, fifteen children were molested, ten women raped, one person murdered by her husband and buried in their basement, kittens and puppies without number were abused, and roughly eighty-percent of the teenage population either fucked or masturbated."

"Headline news is great," Crow cut in, "but it's the obscure little gems that keep us smiling."

"And speaking of headline news," Charlie said, picking up the thread smoothly, "rumors of orgies and Satan worship among Lewiston city council members are greatly exaggerated. However, it is true that the city treasurer is embezzling almost twice her yearly salary, and we here at Dirty Crow radio have obtained video evidence of buggery in the offices of our local police chief."

"Once again, I wish this were television," Greene said.

Joe snickered. Outrageous as the claims were, for some reason he was inclined to believe them. Crow and Greene seemed like the kind of men who might find, and air, real dirt.

"Has a taste for younger cadets, it seems," Crow elaborated.

"Jesus Christ, I hope he doesn't expect them to chase criminals after that," Greene said. "I'll be surprised if that poor guy can walk afterward."

"Oh my God!" Charlie screamed laughter. "Is that a wiffle ball bat?"

"And speaking of cops…," Crow said.

"Let's have it, Little Lisa. Exhibit A coming up," Greene said.

"We have here a wallet belonging to an ex-cop, now a security guard, who had a little pre-show bump-n-grind with our *extremely* underage intern tonight," Crow said, and laughed.

Joe went cold as that girlish giggling filled the cab of his car. "Hey, Joe! Wadaya know?"

"I bet someone is shitting their pants right now," Crow said, his voice bubbling with good humor.

"No worries mate," Greene cut in. "We're not out to get you busted …"

Crow picked up the thread of banter smoothly, "… we just want *you* to know that *we* know. We know who you are. We know where you are. We know what you've done. For the moment, that's enough."

"Yeah," Lisa said, "catch you later, alligator!"

"Indeed," Crow said. "I am very interested in having you on 1200 AM Live – Dirty Crow Radio."

"For now," Greene said, shifting gear, "the show must go on."

"Yes sir!" Crow's voice had picked up a slight buzz, which Joe put down to overuse.

Joe's own throat was dry and constricted. Breathing had become hard, speaking would have been impossible. He stopped in the middle of the road and fished around his back pockets with a shaking hand.

His wallet was gone.

Chirping the Geo's tires, Joe raced down the quarter mile of Railroad Avenue from the cell tower to the underpass and stood on the brakes, sliding to a stop in the gravel and dirt shoulder. The Geo's headlights cast light around the edge of the abutment where he'd had his little bump-n-grind with Giggling Lisa. He jumped from his cruiser, ran to the spot on the abutment's blindside and went to his knees in gravel, dirt, and debris.

He swept his hands over the swatch of ground the glow from his headlights didn't reveal but found nothing. He considered driving the Geo further off-road to use the spotlight, but knew it was no use.

"Fuck!"

Joe stomped back to his car, pissed and scared. All of his money, credit cards, and identification were in the wallet, and now in the hands of the underage girl he'd fucked beneath the underpass. He refused to allow the word rape into his thinking. Two men with sick, perhaps dangerous senses of humor knew who he was, and he had no idea what they intended for him.

And they had as much as promised that they weren't finished with him.

He climbed into the Geo and forced himself to calm down.

Probably just fucking with me.

It was possible, but not certain. If he knew one way or another what to expect from them, he could at least prepare. He didn't know though. Maybe they were bluffing, maybe not. He'd have to keep a lookout.

Groaning, Joe bent down and reached underneath the driver's seat. When he straightened, there was a gun in his beefy hand. It was not his old service pistol, he'd lost that when he'd lost his badge. It was a small 9mm semi-auto, laser sight, full magazine and a round in the chamber.

He reached under again and found his holster, a simple, green canvas thing that he clipped to his belt, before double-checking the safety on the 9mm and shoving it in.

Not only was his equalizer not standard issue for Bailey Security personnel, it was a serious breach of company policy. Termination was a given for any Bailey Security guard caught packing heat.

Under no circumstances are you to engage yourself in a situation dangerous enough to call for a firearm, Mr. Bailey had told him during his orientation on day one. *You're not paid for that, and we're not insured for it. You just keep an eye out and leave the heroics to the real cops.*

Joe had kept his mouth shut. He needed the job after all, but he wasn't playing by those rules.

He felt a little easier in his mind as he went about his route again, shining his spotlight up the road to Crack Town when he passed it. Ahead was the perpetually deserted stretch of pavement that passed an open yard of parked railcars, continuing on to the Western gate of the mill.

Most of the cars had graffiti of some kind on them – *Skuzzbaul Posey!*, *Banger Was Here*, *Topless Is Legal In Canada*, *Eat Pussy!* – but nothing that caught his interest for more than a moment.

"… It was Thanksgiving of 2004," the current 1200 AM Live guest said. "I was only married for a few months and I already wanted to kill the bitch. I mean, she was cool before, up for anything, anytime, anywhere. She couldn't get enough of me!"

"Someone is seeing the past through a pussy tinted lens," Greene commented.

"No, I'm serious," the guest protested. "She was a fucking freak! Then we got married, and it was like she got a permanent rag. All she did was nag and spend my money."

"And feed her swelling ass with a constant stream of Bon Bons and daytime soap operas?" Crow volunteered.

It was hard to tell if he was teasing or commiserating. "Maybe fuck a neighbor or three?"

The guest didn't seem to know how to take Crow's commentary, so he ignored it and plowed on.

Joe saw the gate at the end of Railroad Avenue in the Geo's headlights, and swung the spotlight around, sweeping the ground around it. Not just going through the motions this time, but actually keeping an eye out. Just in case.

"Anyway, it was Thanksgiving, and her fucking family had taken over my house. Her parents, her brother and sister, their husband and wife, and about a dozen little snot rockets. And since they were busy drinking and fighting, I got stuck cooking dinner."

Then the guest laughed, and Joe guessed he was about to get to the meat of his story.

"So, I got the turkey stuffed and ready to cook, and got a funny idea. So, I took it into the pantry and pulled my pants down, slathered my dick with mayo, and fucked the turkey right in its neck hole. It was the best sex of my married life."

A few moments of silence followed this confession, then Crow and Greene both burst out laughing.

"Great feathered balls," Crow shrieked. "Now I've heard it all!"

Greene seemed incapable of speech for the moment.

Encouraged, the guest went on.

"Well, I spooged once, but I was still hard, so I just kept on going." He was starting to laugh a little himself by then. "I busted off three times in that turkey before I lost my wood."

Joe was laughing himself now, his earlier anxieties

almost forgotten. He'd have to remember that trick, maybe for the next Bailey Security potluck.

"Then I cooked it all full of my cock-snot and served it up!"

"How much of it did you eat?" Greene forced out before dissolving into laughter again.

The guest chuckled.

"I had a green salad and dinner rolls. They gobbled that turkey right up though. There wasn't enough for leftovers the next day."

"This guy's a keeper," Crow said, his voice hoarse from laughter, and Joe had just a moment to consider what that meant when he saw the time, and decided he'd better call dispatch with his 2:00 AM report, before she got pissy again.

Joe made his *Nothing new to report*, turned around, and headed back toward the city end of Railroad Avenue. As he neared the dark maze of parked railroad cars, sweeping the spotlight over them, he saw the figure, more shadow than form, dart between two cars at the far end of the yard.

Joe felt a pinprick of fear (*We know where you are*) but shrugged it off and raced to the spot where the figure had been.

Whoever it was, they were gone by the time he reached the spot. Well, maybe gone or maybe not, the railcar yard had a hundred hiding places, none of which he felt like exploring just then.

He walked the outer perimeter of the parked railcars but saw no one. On his way back to the Geo, he spotted a new line of graffiti decorated one of the railcars.

Dirty Crow Radio – Live Tonight in Crack Town.

Below that, flanked by more of the bizarre stick figures, *You Are Invited!*

"Hey," Joe yelled into the maze of empty boxcars. The echo those idle hulks sent back was unnerving. It amplified his voice, and divided it, as if a mob of hidden imitators were calling him out.

Joe kept a hand on his holster as he trotted back to his cruiser.

CHAPTER 5

Joe tuned his radio back to the old stand-by, Coast-To-Coast AM, resolving to leave it there and forget about Dirty Cow Radio and the crazy fuckers who ran it. He'd have to replace his driver's license and cancel his credit cards. The small amount of cash folded into his wallet was gone for good, but he'd deal with it. It was a pain in the ass for sure, but it could be worse.

Art Bell, was on the phone with a man claiming to be Satan. The night before he would have found that mildly amusing, but not after Crow and Greene. It seemed contrived. Lame.

He pushed the laughing voices of Crow and Greene from his memories ear and kept his eyes forward as he rolled beneath the underpass. He'd report the graffiti on his end of shift paperwork, and Bailey would notify the city. It'd be gone by his next shift, if he was lucky. The railcar with its hectoring message would be rolling toward some distant, unknown place soon enough and that would be the end of it.

As long as he never tuned into 1200 AM Live again, that was.

Joe drove his route, working the spotlight and searching the night for would-be vandals and burglars. He avoided looking at Little Lisa's graffiti, and kept his mind mostly on the job for the next hour.

Every now and then though, some bit of the weird but entertaining show would play through his memory …

That's finger banging …

Lisa is the best intern ever …

I fucked the turkey right in its neck hole …

… and Joe would catch himself reaching for the dial again.

Each time that happened, he'd force his hand back to the wheel, cursing his weakening will. Joe had always had poor impulse control, and though he knew that character flaw was at the heart of every serious problem he'd ever found himself in, he'd never cared enough to try to improve it.

At a quarter till three on his radio clock, he pulled over next to the fenced-in propane storage tanks and stepped up to the leaning chain link fence. He unlimbered his prick and forced the arching squirt of urine as far as he could, wetting the hand wheel on the belly of one of the massive tanks. This was one of his foul mood activities that never failed to brighten his night just a little. It did nothing for his mood this night.

He shook off, zipped up, wiped his hands on his uniform pants, and turned back to his car. He paused for a moment, scanning the night around him. He thought he'd heard a whispered voice, faint and unintelligible, but real.

There was no one there. He was alone.

Deciding it was the stress of the night working on his imagination, he stalked around the front of the Geo, slapping the hood and taking some small pleasure from the startling sound. Inside the car again, one hand on the wheel and the other reaching for the shifter, Joe froze.

Don't be such a baby! You know you want to.

This new message was spray-painted across his windshield, a windshield he could swear was clean only moments before as he rounded the front of the car, in drippy, red letters. There were no dancing stick figures this time, no reference to 1200 AM Live, but he knew who had done it. The card he spied stuck beneath his windshield wiper a moment later confirmed the knowledge.

1200 AM Live! With Crow & Greene
A Dirty Crow Radio Production
"Dirty laundry is our specialty
... care to share?"

The company logo was a familiar stick figure, the birdman, caught in some primitive dance, what looked like a hatchet in one hand and a human head in the other. The address, or something close to an address, was scrawled below in tiny, angular letters.

End of 24th Street, Lewiston, ID.

Not wanting to touch the card, Joe turned on the windshield wipers and squirted the glass with wiper fluid to dilute the smearing paint. The card slipped free and fluttered to the ground.

CHAPTER 6

3:00 AM

Joe reached for the radio tuner knob again, but stopped halfway there, seeming caught in the middle of some great struggle. His fingers trembled, his thumb twitched. Static intruded on the normally clear frequency playing on the radio. Somewhere close by in the night, a dog barked, startling him.

Moments later one of the local crazies started up, shouting an obscene sermon to whoever was around and awake to listen.

From somewhere in the darkness, somewhere out of sight, Joe heard the stoned, manic giggling of the little radio slut.

His fingers closed over the dial, and he tuned it back to 1200.

He caught a glimpse of his face in the rear-view mirror when he sat back, and didn't care much for the expression he saw in his reflection.

Not the fear that he had felt earlier, should still be feeling. It was something like excitement. He probed his emotions and discovered that he *was* excited.

"… next segment brought to you by Doodie-Fetish Snuff Films," Crow said.

"Eat shit and die," Greene advised.

"You know what they say – different strokes and all that."

Joe turned the Geo around, pointed it back toward the underpass, seeing, but not registering, that Little Lisa's graffiti was gone. The concrete of the abutment was a weathered but clean gray, as if the red paint had not been there at all.

"I am pleased, if a little leery, to bring you Dirty Crow Radio's Drunk Bitch Friday!"

A loud and wet retching sound blasted from the radio's speakers, and Joe snorted laughter as he slowed, turning onto 24th Street.

"Hey, Lisa," Greene shouted. "Bring in our first drunk bitch!"

"Alas," Crow said in baleful tones, "Lisa is out on necessary Dirty Crow business at the moment …"

Joe climbed a short single lane stretch that twisted an S up a steep incline. At the top, just before the first block of filthy crack-shack houses fronted by junk-filled yards, he found Little Lisa standing by the edge of the road, her thumb stuck out for a ride.

Not at all surprised to see her, Joe turned the radio off and pulled over, unsnapping the clasp on his holster and tugging the tail of his shirt out to cover the gun.

He was unsure of his intentions. Part of his mind insisted

he was only going along with them to get his wallet back and shut them up by any means necessary. Another, deeper voice called bullshit. That voice was eager to go on with them, to spill his dirty secrets, to flaunt them in perfect anonymity.

Joe did have his secrets, and secrets begged to be shared, no matter how dangerous.

Lisa smiled at him and let herself in, giggling her childish giggle. "You know where to go?"

Joe kept his silence and drove on, making a temporary peace between his dueling motives. He'd go where they wanted him to go and see what happened. He'd keep his mind, and his options, open.

For now.

"You know we've been trying to get your attention all night. You're either really stubborn, or really stupid." Now her giggles had an edge, playful and cruel.

Joe slid his hand to his side, felt the hard shape of the gun beneath the untucked shirt, and seized a thin thread of his unraveling control.

"This is because of …," felt his thread of control slip a little, but plowed on. "… what I did earlier."

"You goofy bastard," Lisa snapped, showing, for the first time, an aspect of herself beyond the teasing, slutty teenybopper. "You didn't do anything I didn't *let* you do."

Joe noted her words – *let you do*, not *want you to do* – and wondered if it mattered.

"Then why?"

"Just because," Lisa said, sounding at once amused and exasperated. "Because, because, because, because." Her words melted into laughter. Not the lilting giggles, but manic and shrill.

When she could speak again, she said, "Because Crow and Greene want you. That's all."

"I guess that'll have to do," Joe said, endeavoring to sound accommodating.

Lisa gave him a quick, sharp look, a sly smile that made him uneasy.

Gaunt faces watched their progress through Crack Town, gawking from porches, windows, sidewalks and driveways. Lisa waved at a few of them as they passed. A few waved back.

Past Crack Town, 24th Street steepened, winding through a scattering of scuzzy looking businesses, a repair shop, a run-down bar, and three newer buildings, a mini-storage inside a fenced-in yard. Beyond that, a few houses that had a long-deserted look, a wrecking yard that seemed to stretch out forever to their left, then a lot of ugly, empty nothing.

Finally, they reached the end of the road, a small cul-de-sac before a repeater tower.

Joe pointed to the tower as they rolled to a stop. "That how they hijack their frequency?"

Lisa favored him with a slight, distracted shrug, a movement that might have meant *I don't know*, or *does it matter?* Then, before he could so much as flinch away from her, Lisa's hands slid up his thighs, giving his package a firm squeeze before drawing his zipper down.

Not a good time for this, he thought, riding the edge of panic. Before he could speak a word of protest, her face dropped over his lap, his cock was in her mouth, and he no longer gave a shit.

She really is good at this, he thought, and wondered again just how old she was, and how much practice she'd had. The broken slurping sounds coming from his lap reminded Joe of 1200 AM Live's *Secret Sound …*

Sounds like a blowjob to me …

Letting questions of appropriate times and places and legal ages fly from his mind, Joe reclined against the driver side door and let his fingers slip through Lisa's long hair, curling into loose fists around her tangled locks.

She tilted her head, turning her eyes up to him, and they were not the eyes of Little Lisa, not the bright amber of honey, but bloodshot blue. Her face was pale, dirty. A powder-burned hole marred the skin of her forehead, filled with a jellied scab flecked with some white stuff that might have been flecks of bone or brain. Smears and streaks of dried blood decorated her face like war paint.

Joe screamed in shock and disgust, yanking his hands from her hair. His hands were covered with blood, hair, and shreds of scalp.

The girl's lips curved into a smile around the shaft of his prick, then she closed her eyes and plunged down onto him.

Despite his disgust, he came hard, a rush of horror and lust that he shot down her throat.

When she withdrew, it was not the face of the girl from Boise, the girl from The Doll House. It was the flabby bulldog face of his mother.

Then the wave of pleasure receded, and she was sitting up again – Lisa with the amber eyes - scooting toward the passenger door. He turned to her and found himself looking down the barrel of his gun.

"If it's any consolation, I'm not jailbait. They were only

fucking with you earlier." She winked at him. "Don't guess it matters much to you. Never has before anyway."

"Come on now," he said, struggling to keep a calm voice even as he lunged for the gun.

Lisa did not move, only slipped a finger over the trigger and raised a sardonic eyebrow. A bead of green light pulsed from the laser sight on the underside of the barrel, and Joe could almost feel a pinprick of heat settle between his eyes.

"Easy there, studmuffin. I played nice with you. Now you have to play nice with me." She shoved her door open and fairly jumped from the car, keeping the gun pointed at his chest. "C'mon big guy. They're waiting for us, and we're down to the last hour of the show. Get out and put your hands up."

Joe did what she told him, now regretting, despite the phenomenal blowjob he'd just experienced, not having snuffed her earlier. She'd be floating west away from the city by now, instead of standing there with that crooked grin, holding his own gun on him.

As if reading his thoughts, her smile widened, and she wagged a reproachful finger at him. Then she pointed into the darkness past the tower with the same finger, and he began to walk.

He heard a squawk from the two-way radio in the Geo, then the dispatch bitch's voice falling behind him as he went to meet Crow and Greene.

CHAPTER 7

The walk wasn't long, maybe fifteen minutes from tower to destination, but in the silent darkness it felt longer to Je. He turned back to her several times, hoping – praying – that the silence meant she had gone away. Knowing it wasn't the case, but hope was a troublesome cockroach of an emotion, one that refused to die no matter how many times you stomped on it.

Each time he turned, she followed only a few feet behind. Too close to run for it, too distant to attempt a grab at the gun. Each time she wore a different face and body –the dead fourteen-year-old whore from Boise, his mother, his younger sister as he'd once seen her while hiding inside her closet, watching her as she dressed, her body naked and hairless, the starts of her breasts pointing like tiny hills on the flat terrain of her chest. Once she'd been the eleven-year-old sole survivor of a local sex preda-tor, a man who'd been shanked in prison not long after his incarceration, and how Joe had secretly envied the man with his own private harem locked away in his sub cellar.

That man had even worse impulse control than Joe.

"Don't get too excited," she said from the mouth of the little girl he'd seen on TV. "Fun stuff's done for now."

Not long after that Lisa's lilting voice spoke from behind.

"End of the line, you hunk of burnin' love ya." She giggled again, a sound that still had the power to arouse him.

He stopped and looked around. They were close to the crest of the hill, on the slope facing away from Lewiston. No comforting sight of city lights. The current landscape was all scrub, dust, and dark.

"There's no one here," he said.

"Of course there is, silly man," Lisa said, passing wide on his right, the gun pointed unshaking at his chest, the sprite's grin unflinching on her face. Several paces before him she stopped and bent, one hand sweeping dirt from a scrub-free patch of ground. She stood again with a nod. "Over here big boy. Make yourself useful."

Lisa moved back a step as Joe came forward, bending to see what Lisa had been working on. He found the edge of some wooden thing mostly buried under a thick layer of dust. He brushed more dust away and found a worn corner.

It was a door.

"Go on, open it."

"Are you fucking serious?"

Before he could register the movement, she'd stretched forward and clubbed the back of his head with the butt of his own gun. Light flashed behind his eyelids like high noon and he collapsed forward onto the door. He felt the doorknob, hidden by a tuft of dry thistles, punch into his gut.

Even in his pain and shock, he marveled at the neat trick Lisa had just showed him. Though she'd surged close enough to clock him, and too quickly for him to raise a hand in defense, her feet had never left their spot in the dirt, some five feet distant. She'd simply stretched forward, moving like an illusion.

When Joe thought he could rise without puking, he found her standing as before, one arm crossed beneath her breasts, the other still extended toward him, leveling the gun. The pixyish smile was gone.

"Yes, I'm fucking serious."

Joe settled to his knees and reached carefully through the dying thistle stalks. The knob was surprisingly cold, and he was suddenly afraid of what would be on the other side of it – not dirt, rocks, or squashed and dead weeds, but some great and horrible room filled with monsters, murderers, and …

… Radio equipment?

His grip tightened on the knob, and he wiggled it. "It won't open."

Just as he'd hoped, Lisa did her weird forward lunge.

Joe raised his other hand, a fist in the dirt, and thrust it toward her, releasing a handful of dust and pebbles in her face.

She screamed, a wordless exclamation of shock, or rage, but before she drew back he had her arm, and whatever strange magic she had in her it was no match for his strength. He brought it down over his knee and snapped it like a strip of kindling.

Lisa howled, and as she did her form began to change again, to blur and sag, but before she could turn into the dead girl from The Doll House, or his mother again, he scooped up the gun, put a green dot between her eyes, and blew a hole in her unformed face.

Lisa, the stretched out and blurred version of her, flopped back into the dust, her broken arm falling in a strange, serpentine bend behind her ruined head.

Joe shouted, a sound of surprised glee, and kicked dirt at the inert body.

"You see that?" He shouted at no one, his voice carrying in the still night air. "See that motherfuckers? Leave me the fuck alone or I'll give you the same!"

He stood his ground, chest puffing with his ragged, excited breaths. Waiting for a reply from the empty night.

When the reply came, Joe dropped his gun and screamed, high, frantic, and shrill. The scream of a little girl, or a man who has just been castrated.

He was too preoccupied to notice, or likely care about, the girlish scream.

The hidden door rattled, shaking dust into the air, then flew open, and the thing that came out of it …

Joe turned and ran.

Crow's voice came from close, too close, behind. And from above. "Come on Joe. I've been patient, but you're starting to piss me off!"

Joe pushed himself harder, leaning into his downhill sprint. He was barely holding his thread of control and knew if he lost his grasp on it for even a moment, he was finished. If he didn't end in a headlong roll to the tower below, Crow would get him.

Then something large, sharp, and strong as contracting iron bands closed around his upper arm, and his feet were off the ground, pumping furiously in the air for several seconds before he could force them to still. A skinny leg hanging from wind-blown khaki shorts, human from the knee up, something else from knee to foot, bumped against his face. From knee to ankle was slate gray, segmented, and ended in a bird's talon.

"What?"

"Show's almost over, big guy, and you're tonight's special guest."

Wind buffeted Joe's face, and the night on either side of him was blotted out by the flapping of huge, black wings. He looked up into the downturned face of Mr. Crow. The feathered face and curved beak betrayed no emotion, but there was a flash in the black marble eyes that could have been humor, or maybe just light reflected from the sliver moon.

Crow, Lisa's birdman, lifted him higher, and they turned back toward the door to nowhere. Lisa sat next to it where she'd fallen, shaking her ruined head like a punch-drunk fighter battling weariness.

"No more fucky-sucky for you, mister," she yelled, her voice the indignant caw of an outraged lover.

A last pump of Crow's monster black wings flung them skyward over the open door, then the wings folded down, wrapping the birdman's legs, and Joe's face, in a feathery darkness.

Joe screamed again as they fell toward the door, then through it. His screams continued, though muffled and strangely distorted, like something heard over a weak radio signal.

Lisa crawled into the hole to nowhere, hooking the upright, open door with her good arm before disappearing behind them.

The door slammed shut behind her, cutting Joe's screams off from a world he'd see no more.

CHAPTER 8

4:30 AM

"Dude, the fucking guard's gone." The boy, a pimply youth barely into his teens, had watched Railroad Avenue for the past twenty minutes, waiting for the little Geo the guy drove to hit this end of his route, then turn in the other direction again. That would be their short window of opportunity to get to the pawnshop unseen. Fifteen minutes to get in and get paid, as much cash and goods as they could carry out, including a fine selection of guns they could turn over in short order, and then get the fuck out of Dodge.

But the guard was nowhere to be seen, and now there was the preacher, striding boldly down the tracks and shouting his stoned gospel to the world.

This was good. They could take their time now.

He turned the volume dial on the radio at his feet and lifted it onto his shoulder.

The bass heavy drone of a rap song echoed out into

the dark, providing an interesting backbeat to the preacher's own rap.

"Turn that shit off!" A man stepped up beside the boy, his father maybe, or his uncle, and snatched the radio from his shoulder. He turned the volume down, then moved his face close and worked on the tuner.

A dissonant, wavering bray, part static and a jumble of different styles of music, made the boy flinch.

"Fuck that," he bluffed, but made no move to reclaim the radio.

"… one sick fuck, please give a nice Dirty Crow welcome to 1200 AM Live's special guest, Joe!"

"I love this fucking show," the man said, and started down the slope from the levy toward Railroad Avenue. No need to hurry now that the pain-in-the-ass guard had gone AWOL. "They get some twisted bitches up in there."

The boy followed, pouting. "I fuckin' hate talk radio."

"… tell us about that little girl from The Doll House. The one who didn't get away that night."

"There were five or six of us on the force who knew about the underage whores there. Most were foreigners, some were runaways, some sold or traded for drugs by their parents.

"We had a deal with them. They took care of us, and we took care of them."

"Our Joey always did like 'em fresh," Greene commented.

"Old enough to bleed, as they say," Crow said, then laughed his buzzing, chittery laugh.

"And then one night it all went wrong," Greene said, his tone all sorrow and regret.

"It was Internal Affairs," Joe said. "They found out

what was going on. Not all the details. They didn't know all of our names, but they knew the where and when."

"Come on friend, don't be shy," Crow said. "Tell us how you made sure your little pound-kitten wouldn't turn you in once the state had her."

Joe told his story.

In the world of shock radio, the name Howard Stern is synonymous with God. Even in the backwaters of the Lewiston/Clarkston Valley, where Rush Limbaugh and Michael Savage are considered prophets, many of us have heard of New York City's King of all Media, but until the summer of 2006, I had never actually *heard* him.

I'm not a fan of my local radio stations, but there was one show on a Spokane, Washington station that I liked. The Don and Mike Show, though sometimes a little too political for me at that time, was hugely entertaining. I listened to Don and Mike religiously from noon to four every weekday (their bit with Regis Philbin trying to talk a distraught and gastrically distressed Oprah out of a locked bathroom was hysterical, if you're into toilet humor) until Janet Jackson's nipple caused absolute havoc in the broadcast entertainment world.

The rat bastards at the FCC cracked the whip, stealing much of Don and Mike's creative steam, and shortly thereafter a personal tragedy, the death of Don's wife, brought the show to its knees. With nothing worthwhile on local radio to fall back on, I became a fan of audio books. I could transfer an entire book, hours of audio, onto my MP3 player and beam it to my work truck's radio with an FM transmitter. This solution had its limitations, of course. Audio books are outrageously expensive, and I can only listen to The Dark Tower so many times without burning out on it.

Then one day George Guidall's voice faded out on me, and in its place was a mystery jock casually dropping an f-bomb on this shocked listener, and a guest confessing to having had sex with a ham. I think that was the story anyway. I was laughing so damned hard by then I was ready to pass out.

I parked my truck, listened, and laughed like I hadn't in longer than I could remember. This was the shit. I had no idea who it was or where it came from, and after a few minutes the strange transmission ended, The Gunslinger returned, and I went back to work.

This happened several times over the next few months, and always at the same local truck stop. I was so intrigued by the mystery transmissions I eventually made up an explanation for them, which you have just read. Though Howard Stern is referenced in this final version of *1200 AM Live*, the original version was finished and accepted for publication before I discovered the source of those inspirational, mystery transmissions.

A co-worker, the same guy who introduced me to the music of Rob Zombie and the antics of Don and Mike, brought his fancy new satellite radio setup to work one morning and introduced me to Howard Stern. This was back before your phone was able to stream music, podcasts, and internet radio straight into your car radio or ear holes, and satellite radio consisted of an expensive receiver and antenna setup, and a lot of cords. Those strange transmissions finally began to make sense. The default setting on his Sirius Satellite Radio's transmitter was 88.1, same as the default setting on my work truck's transmitter, and the voices of Howard and his comedy sidekicks, Artie Lange and Robin Quivers, were immediately identifiable.

It doesn't take a genius to see that Andy Crow was inspired by Howard Stern. I am clearly no genius, because I didn't realize it until after this story was written.

Brian Knight

THE AVIAN

Part 2 of the They Call Us Monsters Omnibus

THE AVIAN
BRIAN KNIGHT

Sometimes Jove dreamt of flying, soaring through the window of his little room in Saint Anthony's in the darkest part of night, over the grounds and bell tower, over the wall, and away to a different life. Sometimes he awoke from these dreams with tears on his cheeks, and sometimes he awoke in a vice of guilt and shame, but he always awoke in his own bed, the little black nubs growing out of his shoulder blades twitching as if they still dreamt.

It was Saturday and Jove had no classes that day, so he waited until Father Simon left the rectory and a young priest he didn't recognize replaced the older priest before he went inside to make confession.

It was past noon. Jove hadn't eaten breakfast that day, a self-imposed penance of sorts, and he was bitterly hungry. When fifteen minutes passed on the bell tower clock he climbed down from his perch high up in one of the ground's old oaks.

He mounted the worn and rounded stone steps to the chapel and found it empty, the young priest hidden safely behind the confessional door, the other children eating a late lunch or playing on the grounds.

Jove made his way up the isle between the pews, not breaking the vault-like silence of the chapel. The soles of his shoes against the floor's polished hardwood were silent.

Silence had ever been a talent of his.

It unnerved some people.

The click of the confessional door closing was the priest's first clue that he was not alone. Jove heard his startled gasp through the partition that separated them.

"Bless me Father, for I have sinned. It has been a week since my last confession."

"What have you to confess today, my son?"

There were a number of small things – there always were – but they didn't matter to Jove that day. That day his guilt was focused on one big thing.

"I think I'm turning into a demon."

Flying again, but in daylight this time. Seeing the world through sharp eyes. The sky, blue in the eastern quarter, overcast and gray in the west. Diving to the grass. A worm. Then the worm was gone, and he shot like an arrow to the limbs of one of the grounds many old oaks.

Facing the open window of a classroom, he peered

inside and saw himself sitting forward in his desk, eyes closed, and his chin propped against a relaxed fist…

"Wake up."

The sharp point of a pencil jabbed him in the back, and his perspective changed with a carnival ride vertigo that made his stomach roll. Now he was the boy sitting in his desk, staring through the open window at the large crow perched on the oak outside.

"You'll get in trouble." It was Samuel, the closest thing Jove had to a friend his age in Saint Anthony's.

The girl to their left shushed Samuel.

Sister Lange glared up from a scatter of papers on her desk, then focused on her work again.

Jove chanced another glance through the window.

The bird was gone.

They were growing.

No longer just indistinct black lumps growing from high up on his back, between his shoulder blades and spine, twitching with occasional, tenebrous life. They were slender, leathery appendages, nearly a foot long and curled flat against his back. They flexed and coiled under his shirt. A single claw at the end of each dug lines in his back.

Every night he prayed that the things growing out of him would go away, and every morning he awoke and felt them moving beneath him, growing longer and stronger.

Jove thanked God for the cool spring weather that allowed him to conceal the things beneath his jacket, but he knew that soon they would be too large to hide.

After his last class of the day, Jove escaped the crowded halls between the school and dorm, taking the old footpath behind the building, past the unused football field to the bell tower.

The tower wasn't the oldest structure on the grounds, but it was the oldest looking, virtually unchanged since its erection in the late 1800s. It was also the tallest, the open bell room above the clock face offering a view of the city outside the Saint Anthony ground's walls. The entrance was in the back, and was locked, as always.

No matter, Jove knew where the groundskeeper hid his spare key.

He checked to be sure he was alone before using the key, then slipped quickly inside, locking the door behind him. The ground floor was a storeroom with an assortment of landscaping and gardening tools hung from the wall. A bag of grass seed stood in a corner next to a gas powered weed whacker and lawn mower. Several sacramental candles, some new, some burnt down to stubs, stood on a table next to a logbook. There was no electricity in the tower.

Jove climbed in the dark, round and round, up the spiraling steps until he lost all sense of direction. His shoulder brushed against the bell rope, and he resisted the urge to grasp it. Though the bell operated on a mechanical timer set to the old clock, making the rope a virtually useless appendage, a tug, or even a strong brush against the rope would set the bell ringing. At the top landing, he groped until he felt the rungs of a ladder, then grasped them and began to climb. When Jove ran out of ladder, he pushed a trapdoor open and emerged in a fresh spring breeze blowing through the bell room.

Jove let the trap door drop back and stood, eyes closed, smiling at the sensation of the rushing wind.

It felt like flying.

The things on his back stirred in response.

Without even realizing he meant to do it, Jove shrugged his jacket to the floor, unbuttoned his shirt, and let it slip from his back.

He was skinny, pale, and fine-boned.

The things growing from his back, small black wings with hair-fine feathers that tickled his skin, flexed, stretched, then pumped, as if trying to catch the wind and ride it.

It felt so …

"Nice," Jove whispered.

He let his eyes open again, then retreated into the shadows behind the bell, away from the open window facing the grounds and city beyond.

Anybody could have seen him standing there. They probably couldn't have recognized him, but seen him, certainly.

Inching slowly forward, Jove regarded the grounds, found them nearly deserted, and breathed easier. The few students he did see milling around the common, or hurrying between buildings, were not paying the slightest attention to the tower, so he was sure no one had seen.

He stepped back again, losing his view of the grounds, and turned his eyes to the world beyond the great wall that had held him his entire life.

Seattle.

Jove was eleven years old and had only passed into the

city outside the orphanage gate three times in his life, at least that he could remember.

The buildings beyond were tall and ugly, crowded together and standing sentry over filthy, narrow streets. The city, and the inhabitants he'd seen during his field trips, were frightening but fascinating.

In his dreams he sometimes visited them, though all he could see through their filthy and shattered windows was darkness. Not an absence of light, but of experience. He had no idea of what he might find inside, and not enough imagination to populate the building with even the most basic fantasies.

Jove closed his eyes again, comfortable that none below could see him, and spread his wings.

A tap-tap-tap at Jove's window woke him late in the night and he pushed himself from his mattress with a speed that surprised him. Before his waking mind understood he wasn't dreaming he'd stood, facing his window and staring into the oil black eyes of a dozen birds crowded along his second story window ledge.

Ravens, maybe crows? He didn't know the difference.

They did not take flight as he lowered himself to their level. One of them inched forward and tapped the glass with its beak. Another followed its example.

Jove undid the latch, then eased the window open.

The birds, black as the darkness behind those abandoned city building windows, stepped, hopped, and fluttered inside, landing on his tiny writing desk, the backrest of his chair, his mattress, his shoulders.

One stood on his ink blotter, regarding a postcard image of The Space Needle tacked to his wall with a cocked head.

One of them squawked in his right ear, another in his left, and he hushed them, a finger raised to his lips.

"Shhh, you'll get me in trouble."

They squawked again, though much more quietly, and leapt from his scrawny shoulders, one landing on the sill next to the open window, the other joining those on his desk.

Jove yawned, went back to his bed, and flopped belly first onto his mattress. Sleeping on his back was too uncomfortable these days. The birds on his bed made room for him instead of scattering.

When he awoke the next morning to the six-o-clock bell the window was still open, his room cold, and the birds were gone.

Jove was in a rare mood, lonely and wanting company. After kneeling beside his bed to say his morning prayers, he dressed and walked down the hall to Samuel's room.

He knocked softly at first, whispered his friend's name through the door, and when there was no reply, tried again.

On the other side, he heard the squeaking of bedsprings and the thump of feet on floor. He waited, but Samuel did not answer the door.

"Samuel, you awake?"

Nothing.

Without thinking about what he was doing, Jove

closed his eyes, and after a momentary spinning sensation, light flooded the darkness behind his eyelids.

Morning light.

Standing on a window ledge, he stared through a part in the curtains into Samuel's room, and found the boy sitting on the edge of his bed, frowning at the door.

Samuel shook his head, then lay back down.

Jove closed his eyes again, then opened them, no more than a blink, and faced the hall-side of Samuel's door once more.

Jove walked back to his room, and by the time his door was closed behind him, the desire for company had passed.

"You've lost weight." The nurse, a homely old nun with gray teeth and a large mole on her cheek regarded Jove sternly. "Are you eating?"

"Yes," Jove said, nodding up at her, though in truth he'd skipped lunch that day. The chicken was normally bland to the point of tastelessness, but that day its scent was strong, nauseating.

She looked back at the scale, slid the weight, tapped it with her finger until it balanced again, and frowned.

"You've grown a few inches since your last visit, and you don't look any skinnier." She lifted a clipboard with his chart from a hook on the wall near the scales. "You were ninety-eight pounds two months ago …"

She regarded him again, eyes narrow, alight with a brand of unfocused suspicion of which only adults, in Jove's limited experience anyway, were capable.

"What?"

She sighed and pulled him none too gently from the scales. Her narrow fingers clamped over his shoulders, his wings twitched in response to the pain.

"Stand up straight," she snapped.

"I am," he said, then cried out as she slapped the small of his back with her clipboard.

"Don't contradict me."

Jove sucked in a breath and puffed his chest out, doing his best to hide the newly changed landscape of his back.

They were getting harder to hide.

She made a final note on his chart and tucked the clipboard under her arm. "You can go now."

"How much?" He retreated a step from her returned and newly hardened glare, grabbing blindly at his jacket hanging near the door. "How much do I weigh?"

"The scale's incorrect," she said. "I'll have to recalibrate it."

"How much though," he asked again, almost positive the question would earn him another slap. "I'm just curious."

She sighed again, moving quickly from anger to exasperation. "Seventy-six pounds. But the scale is incorrect."

Jove nodded and slipped his jacket on before turning away from her and leaving the room.

"Charlie, grab that little douche."

Saint Anthony's varsity football team, county champions for the last three years, grew restless in the offseason, so the younger and smaller kids knew to stay away from them when there were no teachers or adults close by.

This went double for Jove and the other orphans, wards of The Church who didn't have any family to report bullies to.

That day, on his daily afternoon pilgrimage to the bell tower, Jove stepped through one of the school's back doors and right into their hands.

There were three of them. Charlie, a starting lineman, a fat second string player whose name Jove didn't know, and a former team member that *everyone* at Saint Anthony's knew, the fallen hero of the Saint Anthony Saints and former starting quarterback, Benson Cochran. Only the teachers called him Benson. To everyone else it was Bennie.

The second stringer leaned against the brick wall, a badly made smoke crumbling between his fat fingers.

Charlie grabbed Jove from behind in a bear hug, pinning his arms to his sides and hoisting him a foot off the ground. Crushing his wings painfully against his back.

Jove cried out and one of Charlie's hands crept up over his mouth.

Bennie laughed.

"C'mon, man, share with the kid now."

The fat boy took a long pull from his joint, leaned in close to Jove, and blew the smoke in his face.

Jove held his breath for as long as he could, but it wasn't long before his burning lungs forced his lips to open and draw in a burning breath, and the big kid blew another cloud of it into his face. It burned his nostrils, made his stomach queasy, his head spin. It was a heavy, pungent odor, a potent mixture of skunk spray and burning leaves.

Bennie plucked the joint from his friend's hand and did the same.

"Don't even think about telling anyone," Charlie whispered into his ear.

Bennie leaned in close, his nose only inches from Jove's. "If we get busted, so do you."

Hurt, panicked, wrapped in a constricting cocoon of smoke and claustrophobia, Jove kicked out. His foot connected with Bennie's crotch and the older boy doubled over with a high-pitched squeal of pain.

Then Jove was airborne, flying over Bennie's crumpled body. He felt a moment of pure joy, pure freedom, before he hit the ground.

He felt, and heard, the snap of his leg bone. The nova burst of pain eclipsed everything for an undeterminable moment, then dimmed to steady, pulsing bursts. The world came back, fuzzy at first, then bright and stark in its clarity.

Charlie and the fat boy stood over him.

"Fuck 'm up," Bennie said, still on the ground behind them, his words little more than a wheeze. "Do it!"

A foot connected with the side of Jove's head and he cried out.

Brightness faded to gray, gray to black.

Then the birds came.

<hr>

Time passed, but not much. Jove's quiet dreams of flight ended, and he opened his eyes on the patch of grass where

Charlie and his friend had stood, ready to beat and kick him.

The older boys were gone now, but the birds were not.

They marched, pecking at the ground, bringing up an occasional worm. One of the big black birds held one out to Jove, and when Jove only stared at it, the bird gulped it down with a casual toss of its feathery head and went in search of more.

Slowly, Jove sat up, wincing in anticipation of the pain in his broken leg.

But there was no pain.

Jove sent an exploring hand across it, and there was no pain, no break.

He stood, and the birds took flight around him, vanishing into the sky.

Jove watched them out of sight.

***

Spring break arrived, and Jove sat in a high bough of his favorite tree, sweating in his jacket while he watched students file out to meet waiting parents. Soon they would all be gone except the orphans.

He watched Samuel leave and resisted the urge to climb down and wish him a happy vacation.

Charlie passed almost beneath him, the older boy still bearing the marks of the bird attack, and marched off the grounds alone. He looked back only once to wave at Bennie.

Bennie, leaning against the school building with his arms crossed. He did not wave back. He hadn't even seen Charlie's farewell.

He watched Jove.

After a while, Bennie, also orphaned and consigned to the care of the church, retreated to the dorms where he would spend his spring break.

When Jove was sure Bennie wasn't simply hiding somewhere nearby and waiting to ambush, he climbed down and walked to his own room, where he planned to read, then sleep.

And maybe, if he awoke sometime in the night, visit the bell tower and spread his wings.

* * *

Jove dreamed of pain, fever, then soaring into the night sky with the cool wind in his face. Exhilaration, a rush of excitement, and the steady whoosh of his wings pumping the air.

His wings. He could see them in his periphery. They were huge, strong, and black as the fine down covering his body. The skin of his hands was thick, leathery; his fingers long and narrow, tipped with inch-long claws. His thighs were muscular, wreathed in a velvety black nap. From the knees down, they were the legs of a monster bird, ending with four-toed talons.

He didn't need to see his head to know that it had changed too. His short black hair was now a crown of feathers, his bland, pale features molded forward and hardened into a beak.

Not a demon.

A bird!

He circled the school grounds, regarding the city beyond with something that was almost hunger, but did not quite dare to cross into the boundary set by Saint Anthony's walled perimeter.

A bird cried out somewhere in the night, and he answered with a shriek that was still half-human.

His spiraling flight closed in on the bell tower, and with a last cry, at once joyous and bestial, he dropped from the sky, folding his wings behind him. He landed on the bell room lattice, his clawed feet gripping the ledge hard enough to gouge wood.

He remained there for a time, silent and still.

The scrape of tiny claws on the bell room's plank floors drew his gaze, keen even in the near perfect darkness, and he leapt, catching the rat with a clawed foot, piercing it, then tossing it into the air in one seamless motion.

He caught it on the fly, the snap of his beak not quite masking the creature's squeals of pain. He felt tiny claws scratch at his throat as he swallowed it whole

Jove watched Seattle's lights from his high perch …

... And awoke the next morning as the bell sounded six o-clock, curled up, naked and shivering on the dusty plank floor of the bell room.

His flesh was hairless and pale. His hands were small and weak, his feet once again only feet.

His wings, though not the powerful, beautiful things he had dreamed them the night before, had grown again, reaching from the tops of his shoulders to the small of his back.

Jove felt a sudden, wild urge to leap from the tower,

and had taken a step toward the inviting, open sky beyond the transom when he spotted something that hadn't been there on any of his previous visits. Something tacked to the wall. A business card, old, bent at the corners, the paper gone yellow with age.

A rough stick figure of a man with an elongated bird's head and wide-spread wings seemed to be caught in a dance on the left side of the card, one foot raised in mid-step. It held a hatchet in one of its hands. The other held what appeared to be a severed human head by its hair, the rough features of the tiny face twisted in a parody of pain. It reminded Jove of Egyptian hieroglyphs he'd seen in a world history book, but he didn't think it was Egyptian.

On the right, next to the dancing stick figure, was a block of text.

1200 AM Live! With Crow & Greene
A Dirty Crow Radio Production
"Dirty laundry is our specialty
... care to share?"

Below this, at the very bottom margin, someone had added a short message in a messy, hurried scrawl. The ink was faded to near illegibility.

Look out for the birdman.

Jove turned it over, compelled despite his unease.

On the back was a newer, neater line written in black ink.

I don't know what this means, Jove, but it came here with you, so I thought you should have it back.

Jove flipped the card over again, studied the prancing stick figure, the birdman.

He didn't know what it meant either.

After a few more moments spent studying the card, he retreated back through the trap door and down the creaking spiral steps instead.

He pulled the old, filthy tarp from the lawnmower, vowing to return it as soon as chance allowed, then wrapped himself and made haste to his room.

He hoped he would make it back before the remaining students, no more than a dozen, took to the hallways.

He did not pray for it though.

Jove was beyond prayer now, and he knew it. Perhaps he had always been.

In the chapel again.

Jove stood before the holy water, hand trembling, braced himself … against pain, burning, instant death? … and extended the index, middle, and ring fingers of his right hand toward it. He hesitated at the last moment, then plunged them in.

There was no pain. No burning or death. Neither was there a feeling of power or blessing. No reason to believe this water was anything more than what ran from the fountains in the hallways of the school, the sprinklers on the ground lawns.

Jove touched his forehead with his wetted fingers and made the sign of the cross. His skin did not burst into flame. No demons fled his body. His wings did not shrivel and fall off.

Jove left the chapel without making confession. There was no need to confess, because there was no sin.

Perhaps, he thought, there is not even God.

Jove could not suppress a stab of superstitious fear and a shudder at the thought, but neither could he suppress the thought.

No sin. No God.

What then?

What was there to believe in?

Jove left the chapel, one riddle solved, at least in his mind, but a greater one now raising a clawed hand from the dungeons of his mind.

Most of the teachers and staff left to visit their own families over the next few days. All that remained was a skeleton crew of orphans with no family to rejoin, and clergy with no life except for the church.

Jove locked himself in his room after eating breakfast and slept the days away, only leaving when the sun dipped into the western horizon, to eat a late dinner and take up his usual post in the bell tower's top room.

Waiting for … something. Anything.

But nothing happened. There was no great change like in his dream. Even his wings had quit growing, and Jove wondered with equal measures of fear and hope, if they would soon begin to wither. Perhaps the holy water had worked, though in a less dramatic fashion than he had anticipated.

They did not shrink. Every sunset when he uncovered them, spreading them to feel out the breeze that whisked through the top room of the tower, they felt stronger, more a part of him. When he flapped them, he was able to raise the dust of years from the plank floor, but there was no way they could support him in the open air, so he didn't try.

Sometimes he heard the birds singing or flapping away in the dark. Sometimes he called them to him with a whistle. Sometimes he closed his eyes and viewed the world through theirs.

On the fourth night, he heard, distantly, a gunshot and a cry of pain. Soon, though not soon enough Jove judged, there were sirens. He scanned the streets visible to him from his perch, even his vision grown keener it seemed, and spotted lights flashing blue and red.

There was a police car, then another, then an ambulance.

He watched them stop at the very building he often visited in his dreams and gasped as a familiar figure stepped from the shadows to greet them.

Father Simon spoke to one of the officers while the others went inside, guns drawn.

The priest shook his head and gestured down an alley, and the officer he spoke with pulled a notebook and scribbled.

Yes, his vision was keener.

The other officers came out of the building a few minutes later, one of them gesturing for the paramedics to follow him inside. They returned shortly, carrying a shrouded body on a stretcher.

Father Simon moved to the rear of the ambulance, and they stopped. After a few seconds of animated conversation, an argument he thought, the priest approached the body and pulled the shroud from its head.

There was a clenching in Jove's chest, a burning in his throat. He understood.

Father Simon, a good man who had always been a friend to Jove, had refused to let them take the dead away until he could give last rites.

Though Jove no longer truly believed in Father Simon's God, the priest had given him something to believe in. The goodness of a man who befriended orphans and spoke words of atonement over dead strangers.

It was a mixed lesson though. Somewhere out there, a killer ran free.

Jove rushed down the tower steps, buttoning his shirt as he moved, and sprinted past the dorm building toward the gate. He caught up to Father Simon as the man came through. He could hear the grating squeal of rusting hinges as the priest closed it behind him.

"Father."

Father Simon twitched at the sound of Jove's voice, then turned slowly, relaxing visibly when he recognized the boy.

"You startled me. What are you doing out?"

Jove's first impulse was to lie, to say the gunshot had awakened him, but he couldn't bring himself to lie to Father Simon. He settled for half the truth.

"I couldn't sleep," he said. "I heard shooting. What happened?"

Father Simon regarded Jove for a few seconds, and

when Jove decided there would be no answer to his query, the priest finally spoke.

"I was out on personal business when I heard the shot." He turned back toward the gate, "I called the police, but they didn't find the shooter."

"Who was shot?"

"A prostitute," the priest said, then sighed. "I'm tired, Jove."

Jove waited for the priest to send him back to his room, and he would go if told. He had never lied to or disobeyed Father Simon, who had been like a father to him.

Father Simon simply said, "Be careful. The night can be dangerous."

Jove nodded again. "I will be."

Then Father Simon strode away.

Jove watched him for a minute.

Father Simon was old, but he held onto the straight-backed dignity of his younger years, a man that exuded confidence and strength.

And goodness.

When the priest was out of sight, Jove debated briefly, he knew he should go back to his room, but he wasn't tired, and his wings twitched beneath the cloth of his shirt, wanting to spread and feel the breeze of the bell tower.

Jove sprinted back toward the tower, feeling a shock of panic when he saw the door at the base open.

I was in a hurry, he reasoned as he stepped inside. *I forgot to close it.*

An alarm sounded in his unconscious, a warning from

some primitive part of the brain, and Jove reacted without thought.

Ducking just in time, he felt the wind as fist swung over his head, tousling his hair.

The second swing came lower, connecting with his temple, and Jove fell to the floor in a haze of pain and confusion.

He heard a voice, familiar and dreaded, say, "you little freak. Wait 'till His Holiness gets a load of this!"

<hr>

When Jove opened his eyes, he was in the bell room looking down, leaning through the open transom, his arms pinned behind his back.

"Wake up, bird-boy." Bennie shook him, forced him a little further over the long drop.

"Let me go!" Jove tried to wrench his arms free, but Bennie's grip was unbreakable.

Bennie laughed at Jove's struggles and shook him harder.

Jove flexed his wings, prepared to unfurl them.

Bennie tightened his grip on Jove's wrists and bent them forward painfully. "Fold those fucking things up or I'll tear your arms off."

Whimpering, Jove complied, though it was an act of will to keep them folded. He often thought they had a mind of their own, something grounded in pure instinct, and they were proving his theory as he concentrated to keep them still. They twitched and jerked against his back.

"Do those things actually work?" Bennie asked. "They don't look big enough to me."

Angry caws filled the sky. Black shapes swarmed outside the tower.

"Call 'em off or I'll drop you."

Jove knew he could call them to his side in a second, though doing so would probably get him dropped to the ground far below, but he had no idea how to make them stay away. They seemed to realize the danger though, and merely circled and cawed.

"I said call them off!"

Jove felt Bennie's grip loosen and jerked his hands free.

"Hey…"

Hands brushed across his wings, fingers digging in their feathers for purchase, but before Bennie could get his grip, Jove fell.

Jove's wings flew open of their own accord, and he beat the air with them, but they only slowed his descent.

The blast of wind filled his ears as he fell, overcoming the sound of his own screams.

He had time for only one thought – *why won't they work?* – before the wind and the fear and the screams ended, and the pain began.

But it was not the broken pain he expected at the end of his fall, the end of his life. It was not the pain of crunched bones, pulverized meat, jellied guts, and scrambled brains.

It was white hot, searing, and quick, and when it was

over, Jove opened his eyes on a cityscape he had only seen in his dreams.

His wings were huge, powerful, his body sleek and tightly muscled. His senses were razor sharp. He did not see or hear, but felt the flock that flew with him, above, below, behind and to his sides.

He was the creature from his dreams, not a boy, not even a bird, but an avian of some kind.

Forgetting the attack in the bell tower, forgetting, temporarily, his life on the ground, Jove gave in to his avian instinct and let his new wings carry him into the Seattle night.

The city was fantastic from above, streets and avenues teeming with life and activity even in the night. Streets and buildings were illuminated, even at the latest hour, by streetlamps and storefront signs, some glowing with the brightest colors his eyes had ever beheld. Swarms of automobiles created their own light, adding to the tapestry of the city.

The light drew Jove down to the high roofline, but he didn't dare fly lower.

He wondered if the people below would flee screaming if he flew down among them, and knew the answer was yes.

He roamed the city for hours, landing on the highest peaks to rest and observe. The falling moon eventually led him back over the deserted streets he knew from his hours in the bell tower, and as the school grounds came into view, Jove's feelings of excitement diminished under the weight of a new understanding.

If he wanted to keep his home at the school and his friendship with Father Simon, he would have to kill Bennie. He knew he could, it would be as easy as plucking him from his room and dropping him from the sky somewhere high above the city, but because he loved the priest, his mentor, and had once even thought to follow in the man's footsteps, he would not kill Bennie.

Something caught Jove's attention, not a sound, not movement, but that screaming alarm somewhere in his primitive self.

Jove tucked his wings and dove to the rooftop of the nearest abandoned building, making barely a sound as he touched down. He fell into a crouch at the roof's ledge and was still. It was not the building he often stared into from his bell tower perch, the one paramedics had carried a murdered prostitute from earlier that night, but the one closest to it.

Jove heard distant voices, two people, men, somewhere below him.

He stepped forward, dropping from the roof. Wings tucked to his side, he cut the air like an arrow for three floors, then spread his wings at the fourth and landed on the window ledge, his talons gouging chips from the old bricks.

"What was that?" A frantic voice from the open window below.

A familiar voice.

"Stop being a twat," Charlie said.

"But we fuckin' shot her! And he saw us!"

A slap sounded from below, loud as a whip-crack.

"Shut the fuck up! His Holiness didn't tell them anything. You would have known if you hadn't run off."

"But … how do you *know*?"

Charlie laughed. "Because Bennie confessed to him before the cops came."

"What?"

"It's funny, actually. If he had just run away and tried to hide like you, Old Father Simon could have turned him in, but if you confess to a priest, they can't say shit to anyone else."

Charlie's friend made a sound, something between a hiss and a whimper. "I don't like it. What if the old guy changes his mind tomorrow and tells anyway?"

A pause, then, "Bennie's handling that. His Holiness won't be around to tell by morning."

"Whadaya mean?"

"Whadaya think I mean?"

There was no reply.

Jove burned, trembled. The bricks below his feet crumbled between his flexing talons.

"There it is again," Charlie's friend shouted, and a moment later two heads poked from the window below him, searching the window of the adjacent building, scanning across to the fire escape.

They did not look up.

They did not see Jove as he spread his wings, releasing the brick ledge.

He dropped down, seizing them by their collars, and pulled them through the window.

Wind screamed in his ears as he exploded upward into the sky.

Below him, Charlie shrieked.

The fat friend made no sound, he dangled limp, unconscious, from Jove's grip.

Jove climbed the sky without looking down.

The city's ambient glow faded behind distance and cloud cover. The air thinned. Charlie's struggles weakened.

With a cry of rage, a cry that sounded more like a caw, Jove flung them.

He watched as they spun and tumbled out of sight, then tucked his wings and dropped like an arrow toward the city below.

<hr>

Jove knew at once that something was wrong.

He saw the crowd gathering from far above the grounds, students and the few remaining teachers, streaming from the dorms to the steps of the chapel.

As he drew closer, he saw what they gathered around.

He shrieked, a horrible, hateful, terrifying screech.

The gathered turned their faces to the sky, the sounds of weeping turning into screams of terror and trampling feet as they fled.

Curses and frantic prayers to Our Father met him as he landed in the square, but he ignored them, ignored the fearful and hateful faces that clung to the fringes of the chapel yard.

He closed the distance to the prone figure at the foot of the chapel steps in gliding leaps.

Father Simon lay face down on the stones, a sticky red halo spreading around him. Jove could tell by the strange shape of his head that it was too late.

Father Simon was gone.

"Bennie," he whispered. The first word he'd spoken in his changed form. His voice didn't sound anything at all like him, but it was at least comprehensible if not completely human. It was high-pitched and grating, like a load of rocks in a squeaky tumbler. He shouted the hated name, and this time there was nothing human in his voice.

More screams erupted in his periphery, and he watched the stragglers flee.

He was alone with the dead.

Alone, except for Bennie, who he knew was somewhere close.

His strange new sixth sense flashed a warning, and Jove took to the air like a bolt of black lightning. His finely tuned senses registered the fading muzzle flash even as a distant pop sounded and a slug chipped the cobble below his feet. A powerful pump of his wings sent him soaring toward the source of the flash, the shadowy bell room at the top of his tower.

Three more pops sounded, three more muzzle flashes silhouetted the figure at the top of the tower.

Jove dodged the first two slugs.

The third slug punched a hole in his arm, then his wing, tearing flesh and scattering feathers.

He screeched in pain, lost control as his wounded wing flopped in the wind behind him. Tilting to the right, he avoided crashing into the tower wall by mere feet. His plummeting course took him toward the dorm building, and he rolled to the left to avoid smashing into it. Already he could feel his flesh mending, the strength flowing back into his crippled wing, but not in time to avoid a rough landing behind the dorm.

He folded his wings behind his back as his taloned feet scraped through the grass, but was unable to stop his breakneck forward motion. He stumbled, sprawling forward with chest-crushing impact, and slid, rolling to a stop at the far end of the building.

The sting of a dozen new injuries assaulted him, but he ignored the pain as well as he could. He lay on his chest, wings limp at his sides and his head twisted uncomfortably to the left. Past the edge of the dorm building, he saw the chapel, and spread out before the steps leading into it, the indistinct silhouette of Father Simon's body. He could feel eyes on him, eyes hidden behind bedroom windows, and heard in the distance behind him the soft sound of footsteps in grass.

Jove closed his eyes, focused his senses on the approaching figure. He could hear Bennie's approach, the spongy sound of shoes pressing green grass, then the dryer rustle as he trod over a dry patch. He could hear the boy's breathing, quick and harsh. He heard the snap of a joint, the creaking of tendons, the whisper of blood flowing beneath his skin.

Then Bennie stopped, even his breathing stopped for a moment, and Jove could almost see him as he leveled his gun for the kill shot.

Jove exploded into motion, gaining the air before Bennie took his shot.

Screams from inside the dorm, a quick flash of a terrified face, a girl he knew from one of his classes. Then he was above the dorm, gliding in a tight loop. Upside down, looking down on Bennie as the boy stood, his eyes still focused on the spot Jove had occupied only a moment before. Quicker than Bennie could follow, quicker than any human eye could track, Jove swooped down behind Bennie and plucked him from the ground.

Bennie screamed as claws tore through his jacket and dug into the meat of his shoulders. He pointed his gun upward, but Jove slapped it away before he could use it again.

Through a chorus of screams and incomprehensibilities, Jove heard one clear question.

"What are you?"

He ignored the question. In truth, he did not know what he was. Demon, angel, monster, it hardly seemed to matter.

He bore Bennie into the air, over the dorm and toward the chapel.

Beyond the ground's high walls police sirens wailed. The waning night flashed with a cacophony of colors, the feverish orange of the coming sunrise, the panic strobe of red and blue from just beyond the front gate.

His time was almost up.

"How would you like to die?"

Bennie seemed incapable of responding. His fingers tugged at the clutching talons buried in his shoulders. He cried out in pain, shrieked in fright.

Such a tough guy, Jove thought bitterly.

"I can make it quick, or slow," he said, and was a little dismayed at himself for knowing that he was now capable of murder. He had killed that night in hot blood, but thought himself incapable of doing so with deliberation. Now he found himself contemplating the ways he could make Bennie suffer, but even his dismay didn't temper his rage.

A spotlight pierced the dawn's low light, stinging Jove's eyes. He flew higher above the grounds to escape it.

Below him, Bennie's screams continued, and in the garble, Jove heard his name.

"Yes?"

"I said I'm sorry! Please let me go!"

"Sorry isn't good enough," Jove said, and was easier in his mind. "Sorry won't bring him back."

Bennie changed tactics, exchanging fear for fury. He renewed his thrashing, tore at Jove's claws, punched out at his legs.

The searchlight swung across them again, and Jove squinted, flying higher still, and as he gained height a sliver of sun showed itself on the eastern horizon. Just a sliver, but as its direct light touched Jove, he felt his strength drain away.

His body weakened as it shrank back to its human form. There was no pain as there had been during his transformation, and it was slower, as if his body loathed giving up its new power.

Anger retreated as he fell, his diminished wings unable to support him.

Claws retracted back into his shrinking toes, and Bennie slipped free of his grip, shrieking as he plummeted.

Jove made no sound as he fell back to earth. He closed his eyes and slipped into comfortable unconsciousness.

His room was dark except for the glow of small LED lights, red, like the eyes of little demons, and silent save for the persistent beep of machines. For a time, he lay awake without being aware that he was awake. It felt more like the continuation of a long, odd dream than consciousness.

He remembered falling, but not landing.

He felt surprisingly well.

There was no pain at all.

He felt … good. Rested, strong, hungry.

Restless.

Wind gusted outside his room's window, and he wondered how high up he was.

Then a door opened, light spilled in from the hallway outside his room, and Jove understood where he was.

He remembered Father Simon, the fight, the fall.

Voices, arguing.

Jove closed his eyes.

"We don't know how he even survived the fall. I'm the boy's doctor, and I'm telling you he's in no condition for an interrogation!"

"That little mutant is a killer. A priest and a boy."

"Allegedly," the doctor asserted, but the other voice pressed on.

"There are a couple other deaths we might be able to hang on him. Two boys, friends of Benson Cochran. We're only waiting for the autopsy results, but they have wounds consistent with those of the Cochran boy."

"Lower your voice in here!" The doctor paused for a moment, then continued in a calmer voice. "I can't explain the, the growths on his back, but I'm telling you it's a physical impossibility. They're not large or strong enough to … hey, you get out!"

A long, long pause, then, "sure boss, whatever you say, but I'm not leaving that hallway until I talk to him."

"Better get comfortable," the doctor said, and shut the door between them.

Jove tensed as the doctor's footsteps grew closer, had to restrain himself from jumping when the man's cold hands grasped his bare shoulders.

"Healed," the doctor whispered. "I'll be damned."

The exploring hands moved down his arms, over his ribs, then gently lifted him onto his side and tugged at one of his wings.

"What are you?"

Jove continued to feign sleep, and the doctor did not ask again.

The doctor lingered in the room for a few minutes. When Jove dared to open his eyes, he saw the man reading a chart in the low light from a bedside lamp. His glasses pulsed with reflected red light from the heart monitor, giving him a demented mad doctor look.

Jove closed his eyes again, drifted.

He awoke the second time to the sound of the door closing and opened his eyes again on an empty room. He sat up, slowly, careful not to pull the electrocardiogram leads stuck to his bare chest, shoulders, and arms. An IV tube trailed from under a strip of tape on one arm. He tore it out with an atavistic grunt, then swung his legs over the side of the bed and craned his neck to peer through the window.

Night again.

Dark outside.

It called to him.

Jove tore the wires from his body, and stood, naked except for a pair of wash-worn pajama bottoms.

The mellow, timed beeps became a panic-shriek.

Jove ran toward the window, arms crossed over his face, and leapt through it.

A rain of shattered glass fell around him as he left the wailing machines and shouting men behind.

Jove had wanted to see The Space Needle since the day Father Simon had returned from a day trip into the city with presents for the orphans, postcards from the port district and trinkets. Father Simon did not have money for larger gifts, but the orphans appreciated the small things.

Jove picked a postcard of The Space Needle because it was the tallest thing he had ever seen, scraping the heavens.

He sat, crouched atop the roof of The Needle's observation deck and watched Seattle's nightlife.

Sometimes he closed his eyes and viewed the world through the eyes of one of his flock.

He would need to feed soon, but for now, he was sated.

Waiting, but for what he did not know.

A scream shattered his fragile tranquility. He did not hear it with his ears, but through the ears of one of his many friends flying over the docks.

With an explosion of motion, Jove took to the sky, leaving a single feather drifting in his wake.

AFTERWORD

Rise of the Manimals

The Avian was kind of a shock to readers who expected a direct sequel to 1200 AM Live, because it was never intended to be a direct sequel. In fact, it wasn't actually intended to be a sequel of any kind.

During the writing of 1200 AM Live I was in what you might call the early stages of my Manimal phase, where I became intrigued by half-human monsters. I blame the later books of Stephen King's Dark Tower series, and his half-human Taheen. I loved the Taheen, and always wished there was more work featuring them. I've used other Manimals in my work. My Phoenix Girls fantasy series has Manimal characters, but I always felt they lent themselves better to works of fantasy than horror, and horror is my primary genre, so I used them sparingly.

Initially this was just another Manimal story, and the monster was only roughly similar to the monster in 1200 AM Live.

This story's first publisher was the one to point out to me that The Avian was in fact a sequel to 1200 AM Live.

Our conversation went a little something like this …

Observant publisher: *You didn't tell me you were writing a sequel to 1200 AM Live. I thought you were sending me a story about rat-monkeys.*

Dumb writer: *This isn't a sequel to 1200 AM Live …*

Observant publisher: *Don't be stupid! Of course it is!*

He was right, of course. I just didn't realize what it was until he pointed it out. Once he pointed it out I went back and reworked the story to strengthen the connection between the two stories, and though I didn't know it at the time, lay the groundwork for a third story.

There is also the tone of The Avian, which couldn't be more different than the joyfully vulgar shenanigans of Andy Crow and Charles Greene. I must have been in a bad mood at the time, or maybe I was just trying to play it straight.

I suspect that the difference is down to my own low-key crisis of faith that I was experiencing at about the same time. The end result of Jove's crisis in The Avian is that he became a monster. The end result of mine was that I became an atheist.

No, I am not drawing in a parallel between the two.

If The Avian was a bit of a downer for you, don't worry. That's not how Jove's story ends, and if you enjoyed the antics of Crow and Greene, then you're in for a treat, because Crow and Greene are back, and shit is about to get weird.

Brian Knight

THEY CALL US MONSTERS

Part 3 of the They Call Us Monsters Omnibus

THEY CALL US MONSTERS

BRIAN KNIGHT

CHAPTER 1

September, 1993.

Charles Greene had a feeling it was going to be an interesting night. It was like a vibe, something that hit him the second he'd stepped out of the van in the dirt parking lot of the little country bar. They were just outside of a little pissant Idaho town, and the second his old boots hit the dirt every bloodshot eye behind the dirty plate glass window turned his way. He half expected them to jump out of their chairs and start barking at him like the territorial two-legged mongrels they were. The thought made him smile, and his smile made most of them turn away from him just as quickly as they had turned toward him.

There was nothing particularly threatening about his smile. Charles knew this because he had done it in the mirror, always careful to avoid looking into his own eyes. Soul searching was not a wise past time for someone with his special talents. He studied the way it changed his face, trying to discover what his smile revealed that so many people found unpleasant. He was honestly baffled.

He knew he wasn't handsome, not even cute. His face was round and homely, a little too big for his head, which in turn seemed slightly too small sitting on his broad shoulders. His lips were full, his mouth wide, his nose bulbous and squashed between round, rosy cheeks. If anything, his smile, which was wide and, he thought, very expressive, made him look slightly daffy. Foolish even. Still, most people couldn't seem to bear it.

Oh well, he though. *Some people have no taste.*

He checked his reflection in the side mirror, again avoiding his eyes, and saw one of his dreads had fallen out of his knitted Tam. The nest of long, black dreads beneath the loose cap gave his short five-foot four-inch frame another three inches before falling back against his neck. The old boots, the ones Jesse James had been buried in, gave him another two.

He'd walked and driven a lot of miles in those boots, had restitched and resoled them many times, but couldn't stand to give them up. The mental image of some grave robber breaking into Mount Olivet Cemetery and digging up Jesse's grave for a souvenir, only to discover a pair of Reeboks slipped over the skeletal feet, never failed to amuse Charles.

He tucked the wayward dread back into his cap, tried his smile on again – he thought it was kind of charming himself – then slammed the van door.

"Back in twenty or less, Andy."

"Do you think this shithole sells Guinness?" Andy called from the cargo area of the large van, an old U-Haul they'd retrofitted for their needs. His voice was high, reedy.

"I sincerely doubt it, Mr. Crow." Charles's voice was deep, smooth. For some reason people always found it strange coming from his homely mouth.

"Rubes," Andy said. "I'll take a Sam Adams then."

"You're a beer snob, you know that?"

"No, son, I have taste buds. If I wanted to drink piss I could do that for free."

Charles laughed, slapped the side of the van as he walked by to let Andy know he was headed in.

Mr. Crow was in a terrible mood that night. He got that way between jobs sometimes. It was pure boredom. Being inactive for too long always did it. He just wasn't happy unless he was working.

If the place, an old and grungy sign over the door identified it as The Empty Saddle, stupid fucking name for a bar Charles thought, stocked Guinness, he'd grab a few cases. Give Andy something tasty to wile away the time until he could work again.

Charles, on the other hand, had no problem with cheap beer. It all got you where you were going in the end.

Charles approached the door, his long strides at odds with his short frame, sweeping the dark lot for signs of trouble but seeing none.

His long coat fanned out behind him, stirring the dust. He pulled the door open, wishing the place had old fashion batwing doors, and he a six-shooter on his hip. He could have been a Rastafarian Jesse James.

Inside the bar, eyes followed him, though much more covertly than before, twitching between him and drinks held in unsteady hands. He smiled again because he enjoyed the effect it had on people, then stepped up to the bar.

"Hidey-ho good neighbor," he said, watching the bartender's eyes widen first in shock at his strange appearance, then narrow again in irritation at the greeting. "Ya'll serve Guinness in these parts?"

"Do I serve what?" Hands planted on the edge of the bar, leaning forward, offensively close. Trying to intimidate.

"That's what I thought," Charles said, sighing. He scanned the signs over the bartender's head for something Andy might be able to stomach but didn't see anything promising.

"How about Sam Adams?" He caught the eye of a pretty little thing with long blonde hair, tight jeans, and not much more than a scrap of shirt sitting a few feet down from him and gave her one of his low wattage smiles. No need to spook the pretty ones away.

"Lager or light," the bartender asked, not bothering to hide his unhappy thoughts about Charles.

"Light? Do I look like I'm on a diet to you?"

The man seemed on the verge of answering when Charles slapped a fifty down on the bar top.

"Tell you what, cowpoke, you fetch me a six-pack and I'll boot-scoot my happy ass on outa here." He gave an exaggerated peek over his shoulder toward the room at large, then turned back to the bartender who was looking back between Charles and the fifty with mixed emotions stamped on his scruffy face. "I don't think I fit in with the locals too well."

He grinned again, and the man stepped back from

him, swiping the proffered bill from the counter and holding it up to the light for a moment.

Then he turned to the pretty thing who had watched the exchange with a drunkenly detached fascination.

These inbred country turds are dumb as rocks, but they pop out some fine looking ladies.

"Mr. Greene," he said, extending a hand toward the pretty country girl. He fixed his eyes on hers, locked with them, and waited with some curiosity to see how long it took to get inside her head.

Not long at all, a few seconds later one of her small hands landed in the empty palm of his large one, and when she drew it back there was a business card in it. She held it up, confused, and read it.

"Dirty Crow productions," he said, once again catching and locking his eyes with hers. "My partner Mr. Crow and I make movies, and a girl who looks as fine as you should be on the big screen."

"Crow and Greene?" She seemed to be coming out of her daze. She looked at the card again, then him. Her lips trembled on the edge of a smile.

"That's me, Mr. Greene." He leaned in a little closer to her. "I'm the good looking one."

"Hey!" A hand fell on his shoulder and pulled him around. A half-dozen of The Empty Saddle's patrons stood, glaring at him with naked hate. A seventh had him by the shoulder and was drawing back a huge fist.

"You don't want to do that son," Charles said, his voice pitched lower than before, trembling on the edge of violence.

The man halted, fist still in the air. His mouth dropped open as Charles found his eyes.

"You might make me angry. You wouldn't like me when I'm angry."

The pretty thang's would be defender simply stared at him for another second, then shook his head as if trying to fight off sleep. "Are you fucking serious?"

Charles rocked back on his heels and began to laugh.

The man let go of his shoulder and stumbled away from him. The girl screamed and ran, disappearing through the door to the lady's room.

Every eye was on him now.

Well fuck, he thought still laughing. *So much for blending in!*

Something slammed down hard on the bar behind him.

"You take it and get the fuck out of here," the bartender said. "We don't …"

"I know, I know," Charles said stifling the last of his giggles and grabbing the six-pack. "You don't cotton to my kind round these here parts. I understand completely."

He spun on his heels and whipped his cap off with his free hand, and a thick nest of dreadlocks tumbled free, the longest of them nearly sweeping the floor as he made a stiff bow, his hat held to his chest.

"Farewell, fine drunken folk of The Empty Saddle! Until I pass this way again!"

Then he marched to the front door, leaving them behind in mingled postures of aggression and confusion.

Ah hell, he thought as renewed giggles escaped his wide grin. *I gotta have some fun.*

He pounded on the side of the van as he made his way to the driver's door, then wrenched it open and leapt inside.

He'd half expected some of them to try and jump him once he was outside. Kind of hoped they would, actually.

"A Mr. Sam Adams is here to see you, boss." He pulled a bottle from the small carton and passed the rest back through the opening to the cargo area.

A black, clawed hand reached from the darkness and took it from him.

"How much trouble did you start this time?" Andy sounded more amused than concerned.

"The troublemaking was minimal, I assure you."

Charles wedged his bottle between his thighs and started the van. As he pulled out onto the highway, he heard Andy pop the cap of his first bottle and guzzle it down.

"Ahhh," an exaggerated sound of pleasure followed by a loud click. "Thanks, Chuck. That hit the spot."

They were barely a half-hour down the narrow highway that followed the Clearwater River west when the real trouble started, trouble in the form of a rapidly approaching car, its blue and red lights flashing.

Charles slowed the van and scooted over onto the narrow shoulder to let it pass, but it didn't pass. It slid in smoothly behind him, the siren warbling loudly for just a second before going silent again.

"I thought you said you behaved in there." Crow spoke from the cargo area, his voice oddly muffled.

"I didn't say that at all," Charles corrected him. "I said I kept the troublemaking to a minimum."

Charles pulled his van tighter to the railing, leaving

the westbound lane mostly clear, then stopped and killed the engine before the asshole behind him could hit the noise again.

He tucked a stray dread back under his cap and peered through the window to watch a tall man in a dust brown uniform climb from the cruiser behind him.

It wasn't a State cop, which was good. Local yokels were less trouble. The car was dark blue with wide yellow stripes down the sides and a big yellow star with the State seal next to the word sheriff. Charles waited, but the sheriff, or maybe just a deputy, stood his ground in front of his ride. A second later Charles thought he understood why. Another car approached, he could hear a faint squealing of tires as it rounded a sharp bend in the road. Deputy Dipshit was waiting for the driver to pass before sticking his ass out in the road.

But the pickup truck didn't pass; it slowed down. There was another faint squeal of rubber on asphalt as it pulled in behind the sheriff's cruiser. Four strapping rednecks bailed from the back of the truck, Charles didn't recognize any of them as belonging to The Empty Saddle, but thought they probably did. Then both doors swung open, two more burly town-boys climbing from either side.

The one on the driver's side was the guy who had tried to fight him, the one on the passenger's side another local deputy. Between them, not climbing from the truck's cab, looking red-faced in the glow of the truck's dome light, was the pretty thang he'd chatted up to the displeasure of The Empty Saddle's mostly male patrons.

The town pump, or someone's little sister.

The girl's knight in shining flannel and deputy #2

looked too much alike not to be brothers. The girl probably belonged to them in one form or another.

With the reinforcements flanking him on either side, the first deputy, or maybe he actually was the sheriff, advanced on the van, his gun drawn.

"Ah shit," Charles said, though his smile didn't fade. "Redneck retribution."

Behind him, Andy chuckled.

"Well, you've been looking for an excuse to spread your wings a bit."

Before Andy could reply, deputy #1 shouted.

"Step out of your vehicle and walk toward me with your hands up!" He pronounced vehicle, *vi-hick-el*.

"Be a good boy now," Andy said from the back. "Do what the nice cop says."

Charles didn't reply. The others were close, only a few feet away from the van's rear doors, and he didn't want to give Andy away. He thought it would be much more interesting if Andy remained a surprise. He caressed the pedals of a small flowering cactus potted on the dashboard, then opened his door, dropping the three feet from the running board to the pavement. He slammed the door shut again before approaching them with raised hands.

"C'mon now, move!" deputy #2 shouted from behind his brother in arms.

When Charles stepped up his pace, hands still in the air and a goofy smile still lingering behind an honest attempt at somberness, deputy #1, Charles saw the name Everett on a tag on his breast pocket, contradicted the second. "Slowly now! Nice and easy greaseball!"

"For the love of Sagan, make your minds up."

"Stop there. That's close enough."

"Told you he was a wise-ass," someone from the Empty Saddle Gang said. "Nothing a good ass-stompin' wouldn't fix."

"This dumb wigger's got more than a stompin' comin' to him," deputy #2 said. "Any city freak tries pickin' up my sister's got ..."

"Shut up, Danny," the lead cop said, his eyes cold and flat, light gray, never leaving Charles's face. They found Charles's eyes, eyes that were sometimes green, sometimes yellow depending on the light you saw them in, and Charles locked onto them, trying to break open those small windows and find the soul behind them. "Conrad, get in that van and take it back to the shop."

His sister, Charles thought. *Makes sense.*

He should have realized that in a town that small she was bound to be closely related to at least one of her Wednesday night bar buddies.

One of them, a squat and muscular man with a pendulous belly that drooped under the hem of his sweaty t-shirt, stepped from the mob and approached Charles.

"Aren't you going to read me my rights?" Charles posed the question to Deputy Everett, but it was Deputy Danny who answered.

"You have the right to eat the peanuts outa' my shit," Deputy Danny said to general laughter. "You have the right to suck Billy Bob's dick."

Deputy Danny nudged the man next to him, a skinny, twitchy guy who blushed bright red (or maybe it was just the flashing red of the cruiser's lights) but laughed along with his friends.

Billy Bob? Are they fucking serious?

"You have the right to get a mud-hole stomped in your

ass," Deputy Danny advised Charles. "Do you understand your fucking rights?"

"Never mind," Charles said. "I'd like to waive my rights."

Conrad turned back to them and laughed as he drew up next to Charles, then lunged at him, bellowing a loud, aggressive "Ahhh!"

"Quit fucking around," Deputy Danny said. "We need to hurry this shit up before someone drives by and sees."

Charles, who could have killed Conrad in a dozen different ways in the few moments it took the man to pass, ignored all of this. He was busy with Deputy Everett, concentrating hard on him. It was like picking a lock; you had to stay silent and focused if you wanted to hear the click when the tumbler finally turned over.

Then there it was. The click. A small part of Charles slipped through the windows of the other man's eyes and made himself at home.

There was a loud grunt of effort as Conrad heaved his ass up into the driver's seat. The van's driver door swung shut with a tinny bang.

Then he screamed.

The laughter from the Empty Saddle Gang dried up at once and five faces turned toward the van in surprise.

Deputy Everett didn't flinch, didn't blink. He stood where he was, his gun still pointed at Charles, but his expression empty.

He wasn't empty. The man's head was actually quite full. He was only confused, stupefied into inaction as certain memories were rearranged, certain tidbits of passing interest to Charles scrutinized.

Deputy Danny and the other man from the cab of the

pickup were twins, not identical but fraternal, and the blonde girl's brothers. Deputy Everett thought they were dickheads, but he was nice to them because he'd been courting their sister for almost two years.

She had let him do a lot of things to her, but would not let him fuck her, even though she had let at least two of her brother's friends, both present at the scene, get in her. She didn't know Everett knew this, they didn't know either, but it was hard to keep secrets in a small town, especially from a man with a badge.

He thought he was close to breaking her down, and he was certain that once he stuck it to her she would forget all about wanting to be with any other man. She would finally agree to marry him, and then, by God and by law, she'd be his, and he'd do whatever he wanted with her whenever he wanted to.

Charles was finished. Deputy Everett was wound tight and ready to go, as soon as Charles let him.

Deputy Danny ran forward, holstered his pistol and fumbled at the lever that released the van's back door. Then he slid it up, and Charles couldn't help a sideways look at the open door.

Andy always made a fantastic entrance.

A giant black shape, something like a giant bird, but also like a man, jumped from the van's open freight door, and Deputy Danny was gone from the scene before he had time to scream. Blood splattered to the ground where he'd stood. A single shoe fell from the sky and landed in it.

A few seconds later there was a distant splash, and the black shape came back into view high overhead, blotting out the moon.

"What the hell!"

"Ninety-nine bottles of beer on the wall," Andy shouted down from the sky as he circled above them. "Ninety-nine bottles of beer!"

"Holy Jesus, help us in our moment of need," cried a frantic voice from the center of the Empty Saddle Gang.

"Shut up! Keep your eyes peeled!"

"If one of those bottles should happen to fall," Andy sang out with obvious enthusiasm.

Charles pulled the cap from his head. This time his tangle of dreadlocks did not fall over his shoulders and down his back. They danced around his head, whipping though the air with terrible, frenetic life. One produced a knife, the last three or four inches wrapped around its plain black handle while another tugged the sheath free and dropped it to the pavement. Another snaked down the back of his long jacket and emerged with a tiny gun.

Charles's ace in the hole, his little Austra .22 short, engraved silver finish, pearl handles. Very pretty. Not a lot of bang, but Charles was a pretty good shot. The living dread that wielded it rose high over his head and two shots punctuated the cries of panic from the Empty Saddle Gang. Two of them fell flopping to the ground, each of them minus one eye.

Andy swooped in low and lifted a second stunned man from the ground. His cry of terror was high, like a woman's.

"Ninety-eight bottles of beer on the wall," Andy concluded, then tore the man's shrieking head off and hurled both pieces of him into the river.

Deputy Everett grinned at Charles, sweat running down his face, and turned to his surviving companion.

"Everett! What ..."

Everett's sidearm made much more noise than Charles's little hide-a-gun, and his aim was almost as good.

The last man standing, poor frightened little Billy Bob, vanished from the neck up, his head becoming a shower of gore that painted the guardrail and the sheriff's cruiser's hood. His body hit the pavement, blood draining from the rough stump of his neck in a small river. His lower jaw was still attached, though broken and crooked, and a scrap of flesh that ended with a mangled ear. His scalp landed on the cruiser's hood like a blood-drenched wig.

Andy dropped from the sky like a black-feathered bullet, landing lightly on his clawed feet beside Charles.

"Come on, admit it," Charles said, having to look almost straight up to see the birdman's inexpressive face. Andrew Crow's eight foot and change frame towered over the shorter man. "You had fun, didn't you?"

Andy looked down at Charles, clicked his beak once in feigned irritation, then began to laugh. "Yeah, I guess I did."

Without prompting, Deputy Everett fired two more shots into the heads of Charles's kills. The back-splash of blood and brains made him look like a badly painted tribesman. Then he walked to the pickup.

The pretty blonde was doubled over in the cab, hiding from the carnage on the other side of the dusty windshield. Deputy Everett opened the door and dragged her out. She screamed, clawed at the hand gripping her wrist, clawed at his face. Blood dribbled from gashes on his cheeks, dripped from the tips of her long fingernails. When she screamed again he holstered his pistol and clamped a hand over her mouth.

When they passed the cruiser, the flashers still painting the night with epileptic, stuttering colors, her eyes found Charles, and Andy. She stiffened in Everett's arms, then went limp.

"You've made her faint, you handsome devil," Charles said, nudging Andy in the side with an elbow. The little gun was not in evidence, but one of his dreads still held the short blade, waving it in dizzying patterns like a knife fighter about to launch a wicked cut and thrust. He bent at the waist and another of his lively dreads plucked the sheath from beside his feet and rammed it over the naked blade. A moment later, the knife was gone, and Charles's dreads composed themselves into a more or less perfect imitation of how hair was supposed to behave. "Where'd my cap go?"

While Charles searched for his hat, Everett lifted the unconscious woman into the back of the van.

Andy watched this impassively.

The large cargo area was almost empty. There was only the girl, the figure of Conrad slumped against the far corner behind the driver's seat, not dead, but unconscious, and a door standing in the center of the floor, held upright by ratchet straps. It was open a crack, and odd light spilled from it into the dark interior.

Everett regarded the woman for a second, turned toward Andy and away quickly, his torso contorting in a violent shiver, then walked to the three corpses bleeding out on the river road. He bent, grabbed one by the heel of a boot, and dragged it toward the guardrail.

Charles appeared at Andy's side, his cap back on, and looked inside. "Ah, you've practiced valuable restraint. Good man, or whatever the hell it is that you are."

Andy slapped the back of Charles's head with a dark, clawed hand, causing him to stumble forward. The dreads, stacked tall beneath the knit cap fell forward over his face.

"Nobody likes a smart ass," Andy said, though the tone of his admonition was somewhat compromised by the rusty chuckle he made when Charles turned toward him, the floppy knit cap loaded with hair covering most of his face.

"I am what I am," Charles said as the hair righted itself atop his head again without his help.

He wasn't afraid of offending Andy. They had worked together for years, made a great team, a productive team, and they always had fun.

What was the point of working for yourself if you couldn't have some fun?

The night's adventure had improved Andy's mood considerably. He could see it in the way his wings twitched against his back, the rapid tapping of his clawed toes against the pavement, an extra little glint in those beady black eyes.

"We taking them both in?" Charles considered his feathered friend with real curiosity. Usually, once the fun was over, Andy was all business. These two warm, unbroken bodies would bring a fine price, especially the girl.

Andy seemed to consider this seriously for a few moments, then shook his head. "Naw, just one this time. We'll hang onto the girl for a while."

"I couldn't agree more with your decision. She's one pretty monkey," Charles said. "As a wise man once said, cash is a sure cure for most of life's problems, but there is only one cure for blue balls."

Charles considered his own words for a moment, then shrugged. "Okay, maybe two, but I know which one I prefer."

Andy had unfolded his wings and crouched slightly, as if about to take flight, but paused to look at Charles. "Who the hell said that?"

"Me! Just now." Charles gave a little bow and waited as Andy gave his wings a single pump, just enough to lift him to the edge of the van's open cargo door.

Inside, Andy tucked them against his back again and ducked low to avoid the ceiling. He walked to the other side, grabbed Conrad by the front of his shirt, and dragged him to the freestanding door, pulling it open.

A twinkling, alien light, like distant stars, spilled through and silhouetted strange shapes within.

Andy hurled Conrad through it one handed and returned to the woman.

"No more pit stops tonight, okay?"

"Also a wise decision, Mr. Crow."

Andy pulled the rolling door down, closing himself off from the outside world, and Charles latched it before checking on Everett one last time, then returning to the waiting cab.

Deputy Everett was struggling to get the third body over the guardrail. He was positively covered in blood now.

Afterward, good old Deputy Everett would drive back to The Empty Saddle, drink a beer, confess to the murders of his friends, The Empty Saddle Gang, and the woman he'd hoped to marry before discovering that she was indeed well on her way to becoming the town pump.

Charles and Andy resumed their westward journey, which would end in Seattle after a few short stops. They would set up shop there for a while, then head south to California.

There were a lot of empty, boring miles between here and there, and Charles was glad they'd have some company on the way.

CHAPTER 2

August, 2009.

Doug Oleander, American Star ace reporter and fiction writer – on most days the two were one and the same - considered his blank notebook page for a minute, unsmiling, his face mute of all expression. The sinking Las Vegas sun glared through the blinds covering his wide window, throwing hard bars of light across the dark surfaces of his living room. He tapped the point of his pen absently against the blotter with his right hand, adding to a confusion of blue freckles. With his left he scattered and sifted through a collection of 3x5 photographs he'd been sent over the past few weeks, hoping something would reach out and tweak his imagination.

Smoke drifted from the cigarette clamped between his lips, creating ghost-shadows across his desk, burning his eyes. The aroma of fresh-brewed coffee (French Vanilla, his favorite, what his ex-wife once referred to as his faggot coffee) teased him.

Then he stopped, isolating a single photo from the collage of images.

Damn good Photoshop, he thought.

The photo was a little fuzzy, a little blurred. It looked like someone had snapped it through a pane of dusty glass. The object of the photo was just out of focus enough that you couldn't make out any of its features.

"Not bad," he said aloud, leaning so close to it that his nose almost touched the glossy surface. Somehow it didn't feel like a fake. A fake wouldn't have been so ambiguous.

Not that it mattered to him one way or the other. What mattered to him was that, despite the overall poor quality of the photo, it was strange enough to capture the imagination.

He flipped it over and read the note scrawled in labored and minuscule writing on the back.

Mr. Scott. Am a BIG fan. Think you're a brave and groundbreaking journalist. Was on vacation to see my daughter in Seattle when I saw this. Picture taken from the Sky City restaurant at the top of the Space Needle. Man at another table saw it too and says others have seen it. They call it The Puget Devil. He said it's killed people. Worried about my daughter. Please investigate.

With love and respect.

Margie Vasquez

. . .

Doug's overall opinion of his readers was low. They were, in fact, made up mostly of gullible morons and paranoids, but they always came through for him in a pinch, God bless them.

Some of his excitement drained away when he saw Margie had neglected to leave him a phone number or email address. Following directions wasn't a strong suit for the Margie Vasquez's of the world. She had at least followed his admonition, printed at the bottom of each piece he published in the Star, to confine any communiqués concerning reader submitted photos to the back of the photos. It kept their reader submissions from turning into ten-page handwritten life stories. He sifted through the pile of open envelopes until he found hers.

With the envelope in hand, he spun in his chair and rolled over to his computer station. A quick search found a phone number for a Margie Vasquez in Mountainhome, Idaho, and scribbled it down on the back of the envelope.

As long as I'm here, he thought, and did a Google search for Puget Devil.

He found nothing. If this Puget Devil was some kind of Seattle urban legend, then it looked like he was getting first shot at covering it.

He wondered if he should try to copyright "Puget Devil," make the damn thing his property and keep the other bizarro gossip rags from using the name. He decided he'd hold off until it seemed likely the story would grow legs enough to run.

He smiled, spinning back to his writing desk, and scooped the rest of the photos and their accompanying envelopes back into an open desk drawer.

After a quick call to Margie Vasquez, who was *thrilled – nay, honored* to speak with him, Doug started a folder on The Puget Devil. The new project folder looked flat and pointless, as they always did to begin with, containing only a few scribbled notes, a sheet with a few phone numbers – Margie's daughter and the gentleman they'd met at Sky City, and the photograph, tucked back into its envelope.

In a few week's time it would fatten up as he added all the handwritten first drafts and printed final drafts of his Puget Devil series, which he hoped would be a long one. From his admittedly obscured vantage point, this story seemed to have potential, all the ghoulish glamour of Bat Boy and Jake the Alligator Boy, with a little bit of Satan thrown in.

He moved the pen over a blank notebook page and scratched out the title and byline.

Good shit, he thought.

He killed the remainder of a smoke in one long draw and chased it down with a swig of his *faggot coffee*.

The smile on his face broadened as he began to write again.

Doug loved his job.

He was having fun.

Monster Stalks Seattle!
By Ty Scott

Nobody knows where it came from, nobody knows what it is, but the monster known locally as The Puget Devil has terrorized the citizens of Seattle, Washington for months, maiming and killing, feeding on the dregs of Emerald City society.

The Puget Devil's preferred victims are prostitutes, drug abusers, and vagrants, people referred to by criminologists as Less Dead. Just like most serial killers of our time, this inhuman winged killer preys on the fringe, which is perhaps why Seattle law enforcement officials have made no effort at all to stop the monster.

This reporter's initial attempts to interview Seattle's top law enforcement officials about The Puget Devil were unsuccessful. However, with sightings and body counts on the rise, I dare say the opportunity for an *American Star* exclusive will present itself in time.

"This is only another sign of terrifying days and events to come," says *American Star* theological expert, Father Randal Rhodes. "With the recent appearance of the bleeding Virgin Mary in the Holy City, and the now world-famous image of Jesus weeping on a taco chip in New Mexico ..."

When Doug finished with the typed second draft two hours later on his laptop, the sun's last light cast a burnt umber glow around the city skyline through his window. He was pleasantly spliffed by then and enjoying the combined aroma of French vanilla coffee and some really fine herb. The nod to his Weeping Jesus Taco Chip story from a few months back had been an inspired goof, and an excellent opportunity to bring his recurring theological expert back for a quick appearance. His editor was afraid that someone would eventually recognize the name as belonging to the long-deceased Ozzy Osbourne guitarist. Doug privately hoped someone would. He'd written his expose on Randal Rhodes – *Ozzy Guitarist Faked Death! Alive and Well in Mexican Monastery!* - years ago. It was in his Randal Rhodes folder, along with every expert opinion old Randy had ever offered Doug in his years working for The Star.

If he didn't let himself get lazy he'd have the piece wrapped up that night, then off to the editors, along with a scanned copy of the photo that had inspired the night's work.

Should call the Seattle Police first, Doug thought. Get their *No Comment* before typing out his final draft. Then at least one thing about the story would be true and he'd be able to go to bed that night with a clear conscious.

If his calls to the Vasquez daughter and their Sky City acquaintance proved inspiring, maybe he'd get a very early start on the next installment, assuming his editors even liked the first one enough to print it.

After ten years working with them, the first four as a freelancer, the past six on staff, he knew their tastes pretty well. If he got enough real people to talk about the Puget Devil, he could keep it going for a while.

He needed more photographs though. That blurry snapshot would be enough to pique the buyer's interest for the first issue, maybe a second, but eventually people always wanted something more, something better.

That was for later though. If the Puget Devil turned out to be a winner, he'd do a talent search of the Seattle area. Just about anyone with a camera and a computer could do the work he needed. If he found someone with a little freelance graphic art experience, he'd be set.

Doug Oleander sipped his coffee and packed more herb into the bowl of his bong. Sometimes a story turned out so well, you had to celebrate twice.

His editor loved the story.

The man's return email was in Doug's inbox the next morning. It was brief, almost stark, but he found almost nothing at all about the piece to complain about, not even the return of Father Rhodes, which was as close to a rave as Doug ever got from the man. His one complaint, and Doug had expected it, was about the quality of the accompanying photograph.

Too fucking grainy. If you're trying to inspire nostalgia for the golden days of alternative journalism in our readers, then stop it. No one gives a shit about the good old days.

. . .

"Sour old fuck," Doug said, printing off a copy of the email to store in his Puget Devil file. But the sour old fuck was right.

Doug drafted a quick response, telling him the photo was an unaltered (by him at least) reader submission, and that if The Star wanted The Puget Devil to be a regular he would hire someone in Seattle to produce a few quality shots.

He sent the email, printed a copy, clipped it to the printout of his editor's original email, and filed them. He tapped out the remains of his morning smoke and made his way to the shower, shedding cloths as he walked and stuffing them into wicker hamper in the hallway.

One of the best things about living alone was that he could walk around bare-ass naked if he wanted to and nobody could complain.

He stood under the hot spray of water for a long time, letting it invigorate him. Mornings were tough. He fucking hated them, but if he let himself get in the habit of sleeping late he'd never get anything done. The freedom to be as lazy as you wanted was both the blessing and the curse of working from home, and he'd fallen into that bad habit before.

Ten minutes later, showered, dried, wearing only an old pair of boxers, Doug shambled into the kitchen and started a pot of coffee. His computer sounded out in his office/living room, telling him he had new email, but coffee would have to come first.

When he finally made it back to his desk, the email from his editor said pretty much what he'd expected. Hire a freelancer to produce better photos, fine, but it was coming out of his pocket. No surprise at all, and it meant the old bastard liked the first story enough to run a second.

He replied, printed copies of both new emails, put them in the folder.

It was just after nine in the morning.

Doug decided to give himself until noon to work on his novel, the masterpiece that would make him better known than Ty Scott, his American Star byline. The working title was *The Adventures of an All-American Lesbian*, but that would change when he thought of something more marketable. It was a roman à clef type story, ala The Valley of the Dolls or Primary Colors, about a young Hollywood actress whose excesses lead to addiction and committal, and whose return to happiness and sanity is precipitated by a lesbian affair with one of her fellow loony-bin inmates.

Of course, the book was about no one, but there were enough crazy young celebutards, most of whom had dabbled in the love that dare not speak its name – these days lesbianism was as much a fashion statement as tramp stamps and straight hair – that anyone who read his book could make almost endless speculations about the identity of his young and endlessly horny protagonist.

And now that he finally had an agent interested in the project, for both the book and film rights, he thought it had an excellent chance of breaking through.

The going was slow though. Making stories up for The Star was easy, but *The Adventures of an All-American Lesbian* was harder than he had imagined. The novel's readers were apt to be a lot smarter than his American Star readers, so he had to make the shit he invented sound real, or at least plausible. He couldn't count on Father

Randal Rhodes to bail his ass out of a moral dilemma, or the Weeping Jesus Taco Chip to inspire a sense of profundity.

As for The Puget Devil, that kind of shit would get him laughed out of the business, which was why he published his American Star stories under a pen name. Shit like that just did not happen in real life.

Doug pressed bravely forward, deciding to spice up the rather dull chapter he was working on with a three-way between his protagonist, her psychotic lover, and an orderly.

Noon arrived at last, the three hours had dragged out and felt more like six, but the chapter was finished, and that three-way had managed to raise a respectable pup tent in the lap of his boxers, so he thought it was probably a success.

He turned his email back on, he kept it off while working on the novel, he didn't need the extra distraction, and found one new email, from his ex-wife.

He checked the date on the calendar over his desk, Garrison Girls, nude British army wives of 2009, and saw it was about that time of month. The bitch would be *thanking him* – har, har, har – for his monthly alimony payment. He replied with a brief but heartfelt *Go Fuck Yourself*, then logged onto the Seattle-Tacoma area Craigslist and browsed the Art/Media/Design thread. As he'd expected, there were a lot of photographers and artists in need of work. He could be just about as goddamned picky as he wanted to be.

He made his *Artist/Photographer Needed* post, keeping it short and sweet.

Seattle area Photographer/Artist needed for freelance work to appear in national publication. Reply with one photograph and one example of your art. Realism is vital! Will discuss payment upon hiring.

Once he'd set that ball rolling, Doug opened his Puget Devil file and removed the sheet with the contact numbers for Vasquez's daughter and their gentleman acquaintance. Then he remembered that he had planned on calling the Seattle PD before sending his story off, and decided he'd better log their *No Comment* before he did anything else.

All in all, he had a busy day to look forward to, but busy wasn't a bad thing. Staying busy meant food on the table, a modest roof over his head, and his weekly trip down the strip.

Of course, that would change when his lesbian love story hit big. He could kiss the modest digs goodbye for a start and make his trips down the strip a nightly rather than weekly diversion.

One had to hold out hope, otherwise what was the point in trying?

CHAPTER 3

Jove waited out Seattle's last daylight hour in the city's old underground, what once *had been* the city before fire had destroyed twenty-five blocks of it over a hundred years before. The post 1898 city, the modern Seattle, stood seventeen feet above the ruins of the old, and though they had tried to close off the old rooms and sidewalks to vagrants and scum like him, many of them did find their way in.

A small part of the old underground had been restored, there were guided tours, lots of noisy, laughing visitors snapping pictures of the quaint and antique rooms, vaults and passages, but they never came to his part of the old city.

They said it was unsafe, and in more than one way, and Jove supposed they were right, but for him it was safer than the streets, safer than the orphanages, safer than the world of people above him.

Jove had been kidnapped twice in the two years since he ran away from Saint Anthony's orphanage and school, both times during the day, when hunger or loneliness had driven him from the safety of the underground. One was a homeless pervert who had taken him to a tent city in a small forest by the beltway. The other was a rich pervert who had lured him into an old black car with tinted windows, promising food and soda pop and a little friendly company. Neither man lived long enough to regret their actions, but Jove wasn't anxious to relive the experience.

He'd killed the homeless man with his own knife, spotting it on his hip and sticking him in the neck with it in his tent. The rich man had locked him in the trunk of his car and driven around until dark, Jove thought so the man could take him inside after his servants left. He had the surprise of a lifetime when he had opened the trunk again.

Of course, a little boy alone, out in the world above at night could expect no better, but the night was Jove's friend. Since he'd left the orphanage, the kind of men who would kidnap homeless boys and girls had found their hunts much more dangerous.

Jove, a scrawny fifteen-year-old boy with long black hair and a narrow, pale face, slept in a nest of filthy blankets he'd scavenged in his night time ventures into the city. He had no light, but needed none. His night vision was superb. He had no comforts, but had long learned to live without them. He could count his personal possessions on his fingers, but they didn't mean much to him. He had a comic book he'd found one night on the sidewalk, about an old-west guy called Jonah Hex, he had a canteen full of water that tended to go stale, because he rarely fed or drank during the day. He had a long coat with a hood, he'd taken that from the homeless pervert's tent after knifing him, and a pair of old sweatpants he'd cut off at the knees, which was all the clothing he wore at night. He had an old sweater that was too tight on him, and a pair of green, stained pants that were too long, and so baggy he used a rope to hold them up.

The only two possessions that meant much to him, he kept in an old cigar box he'd found in the underground. One was a postcard, old and dog-eared, of the Space Needle. The other was a small business card, so old the paper had yellowed, and bent in the middle. The card had come from his mother, who had died when he was born.

Its most notable feature was a stick figure man with an elongated bird's head and wide spread wings, dancing on the left side of the card. It held a hatchet in one hand, a severed human head in the other.

On the right-hand side of the card, parallel with the dancing birdman, was a block of cartoonish text.

1200 AM Live! With Crow & Greene
A Dirty Crow Radio Production
"Dirty laundry is our specialty
... care to share?"

Below that message, handwritten in the bottom margin and faded to near illegibility ...

Look out for the birdman.

He kept this card because he was sure it had come from his mother, the handwritten warning at the bottom her final words in this world. Whether a warning to him, or just an aberrant last thought written down for posterity before madness and death took her, he didn't know.

He had no doubt who the dancing stick figure depicted, but the man … birdman had never come looking for him.

He must be long gone, maybe even dead by now.

Jove had his small domain, what had once been a storeroom, and the other vagrants who knew the ways down below also knew to stay away from his den.

Jove did not so much live down below during the daylight hours, as exist, and though his place below was well insulated from the inhospitable light of day, he always knew when the day was at its end and the sun had set.

The night was when he truly lived.

It was summer, but the corridors under the city were chilly, the air itself not humid, but downright damp. He guessed it had rained that day, was maybe still raining. He left the deep darkness of his den behind and followed one of the familiar corridors just under the surface, beneath the sidewalks where strips of thick glass bricks in the concrete shed meager electric light down on him.

He'd left his long coat behind, and shivered a little in the chill. The things on his back, narrow black appendages that grew between his shoulder blades and folded against his back, twitched, then unfurled and spread, as if in mounting anticipation of Seattle's dark night sky.

Jove had always thought they had a mind of their own, something rooted deeply in pure instinct rather than conscious thought. He could control them, just like his arms or legs, but sometimes they acted independently.

He let them flap a few times, too small and weak to do more than stir the air a little, then folded them back against his shoulders.

He could hear the muted thunder that meant he was close to the transit tunnel. As always, the sound made him feel like breaking into a run. He held back, not wanting his other side to take control until the right moment. He still didn't fully trust the other side of himself.

Minutes later he found the narrow passage into the transit tunnel.

He sniffed the air. Yes, it had rained earlier, but wasn't now. He could hear the train approaching, could feel it vibrating the ground beneath his feet. He pressed himself against the wall, making himself as flat and small against it as possible.

The vibrations grew stronger, the rumble louder. His senses spiked, his muscles tensed. His body knew what the sound and growing tremors meant, and was eager. Anticipating the change. Wanting it.

Then Jove saw the approaching train and felt a moment of fear at its approach, the fear a small animal must feel when confronted in the road by some rolling steel monster with bright, electric eyes and a mechanical growl.

Then it was passing him at what seemed to be an unimaginable speed. It stirred the air around him, pulling his long, uncombed hair in its wake. When it finally passed him, he jumped away from the wall and ran after it.

He chased it, and at first it drew away from him as if he were standing still. Then the familiar, pleasurable pain ripped through his body. It tickled and burned at the same time, stretched and distorted. He stumbled and almost fell as his legs lengthened, throwing off his stride.

The train, racing onward ahead of him, was closer now. He was catching up to it.

His bare feet, toughened and calloused from going barefoot for most of the last two years, changed, grew talons that scraped the ground as he raced down the tunnel. The things on his back were no longer narrow and feeble.

He spread his wings wide as he leapt from the ground, and he was no longer running, but flying after the great metal snake.

A further freshening of the air told him the South Portal was close. In a few moments the train would leave the tunnel and emerge into the world above.

Jove pushed himself faster, now he could see the back of someone's head in the rear compartment window, and when the train finally reached the open, Jove only feet behind it, the head turned, and a woman gaped at him.

Then he was out, soaring high above South Portal.

Seattle lay below him. The Emerald City, full of life and energy, even after the sun went down.

It was the nighttime city that Jove loved, and sometimes protected.

The city was full of people, and not all of them were good.

I'm hungry, Jove thought, and the thought made him happy. Not happy because he enjoyed hunger, but because of his ability to think at all, to remain fully himself when wearing this strange nighttime body. It was a new thing, evolving a little at a time.

He had always been there, always aware of his nightly adventures, and sometimes mishaps, and he usually remembered it clearly afterward. He'd never been fully in control though. He had become co-pilot to some kind of animal instinct, an instinct so sharp it was almost a new sense. He recognized this animal side to himself, knew it was his only friend, but also knew it was an amoral one. It was a thing that cared only for their shared body, their shared sensations and hungers. Without Jove to temper it, this thing would happily pluck a baby from its mother's arms and carry it away to one of the city's high concrete and glass peaks to eat it.

It was not cruel, not evil, just animal.

Hungry, it said, begged, pleaded. *I'm hungry*!

Soon, Jove told it. *Not now, but soon.*

The animal moved back into his empty belly and grumbled.

This had become a nightly exercise for Jove, to hold his animal self back, to rein it in despite its hunger. To stay in control.

And it was working.

Hungry!

He leapt from his perch atop the black Columbia Center building, taking to the air before he'd known he meant to.

Hungry.

Hunting.

As always, instinct won out in the end, but this didn't worry him anymore. If he had learned anything in the past few years, it was that instinct was useful. To deny instinct, as he had the times he'd gone above in the daylight, was to deny survival.

Jove no longer tried to deny his animal side, only to temper it with his humanity, and it was working.

Jove altered his course away from the bright lights of the city. He closed his eyes as he glided out over the water, sensing the little ones all around, his friends, the night birds. He saw through their eyes, felt the world through their senses. They showed him where he might find a few fish feeding close to the surface of the water.

He opened his eyes and dove.

Once fed, the animal was contented, happy to let Jove do his own thing for a while, and Jove's favorite thing was to visit The Space Needle. He liked to stand above the observation deck and just watch the colorful, glowing life below.

It wasn't as tall as the black tower, but the view was better, unimpeded by the other towers that dominated the southern skyline. When he wanted a closer look at the people below, his little friends were always around to lend him an eye.

Sometimes his instinct nudged him, suggested he have a peek down some dark alley or dock, and it was at these moments, when his animal side seemed almost welded to the morals of his previous life, that he flew down into the city to join its human life, to intervene in the unholy war between human predators and their prey.

It didn't happen every night, not even most nights, but it happened enough for the people of the city to know that something inhuman was among them. It was dangerous, he knew that, instinct and his own good sense told him there was safety in anonymity, but he couldn't stop himself.

He thought Father Simon, the priest who had raised him inside the walls of Saint Anthony's, would have understood, probably approved if he was still alive.

It seemed this night would be one of those nights.

He closed his eyes and found one of his little friends in an empty parking lot below. Mostly empty. It had been scavenging a dried piece of hotdog bun and a few stale chips from the bushes bordering an apartment building when it heard the screaming.

It left its stale meal behind and took flight toward the sound. Next there were sirens, then a gunshot and a mortal cry as someone died.

Jove dove from the observation deck, straight down without unfurling his wings, parting the air like an arrow. He let gravity build his speed before spreading his wings to sail.

He didn't have far to go, and finding the place wouldn't be hard.

Dangerous, the animal reminded him. *Cops. Guns.*

It wanted him to turn back, to find a safe place away from the flashing lights and the new bullhorn voice. He wanted the same thing, to see but not be seen, to find food, to fly over the beautiful cityscape.

Something else compelled him forward.

Not God. Surely not God. Jove had quit believing in Father Simon's God a long time ago, and even if God did exist, surely He would have nothing to do with a creature like Jove.

Not God compelling him, but something.

———

It was a 7-Eleven, one he'd visited before in daylight. His keen black eyes saw everything from the darkness above.

There was blood on the floor, though the body it ran from lay out of view in the snack food isle. A candy bar lay in the wide stream.

There were cars in the parking lot, facing the entrance in a semi-circle, lights flashing, doors open to shield the uniformed men who crouched or stood behind them with guns drawn.

There were two living people just inside the glass door, one a woman with a uniform smock and a look that went beyond terror, something like resignation, on her brown face. The other was a man. He stood behind her, held her by the neck, pressing the barrel of his gun against the back of her head. His mouth was open, shouting, rotting teeth gnashing the angry words he spit at the police. There was no fear in his eyes, only a kind of insane glee.

He would shoot the woman, and happily.

He was only waiting for an excuse, a reason to justify it to himself.

Jove had seen all he needed.

He dove again, leveling off only when he was close

enough to the pavement for his knees to scrape it. Shouts sounded behind him. The cops had seen him now, and in a second, they would recognize him. He pulled up a second before he would have hit the door and landed lightly on his feet only inches from it.

The angry junky smile froze, the wild bloodshot eyes widening in confusion as Jove tore the door from its hinges and threw it aside. It shattered, and behind him someone fired a shot in reflex. A moment later the junky lunatic's gun followed the door into the parking lot, and as the woman fainted, Jove rose into the air again. The shrieking man dangled from his talons. Talons impaled his shoulders as Jove tightened his grip and rose skyward, more shots following him into the sky.

Hungry, the animal said again, smelling the blood, the fresh living meat.

No, Jove told it. *People aren't for eating.*

That was one boundary he'd promised himself he'd never cross, but Jove would gladly give the animal in him its second favorite thing.

He rose higher, higher, until the flashing lights faded to points and the cars below looked like bugs. He rose until the air grew thin and chilly, and the man's struggles weakened.

Then Jove dropped him and hovered, watching as the rag doll figure fell from sight.

It wasn't until he spread his wings wide again and lay flat to glide back toward the city that he noticed he'd been shot, but by the time he'd resumed his perch on the black Columbia Center tower, his wound was healed.

Jove realized as he crouched, waiting for the next thing to happen or not happen, that his nightlife might become more difficult now that the cops had seen him. After the murders at Saint Anthony's, the cops had only known about a boy, an orphan with strange deformities, things that looked like wings but couldn't possibly have been. That boy had been underground since then, and while the Bird Boy of Saint Anthony's was probably a good story they told new kids now to wind them up, most probably didn't seriously believe in him.

Now they would.

They might even connect him with Seattle's latest urban legend, a name he'd heard half a dozen times in his nocturnal wanderings over the past few months.

The Puget Devil.

He supposed it didn't matter. He would continue, just as the monsters he hunted continued, and he would be seen again. There was no doubt about it. Maybe someday they would catch him, or kill him. When that happened maybe he would find out that he *was* the demon he once thought he'd become, back in the days when he believed in such things. More likely he'd just vanish into the great blank nothing, like billions before him.

At that moment, the only thing that mattered was the rising color on the eastern horizon, a violet glow that would soon turn deep red, then orange, then, as the sun finally crested, blinding white.

His time was nearly over, and he looked forward to the rest.

He dropped from the tower, unfolding his wings almost as an afterthought, and caught a breeze that carried him out toward the open water. He'd try to catch a bite to eat before following the early morning train through the North Portal and back into the underground.

As he drifted on the wind he caught his mind wandering back to his time at Saint Anthony's, not thinking about Father Simon, as was most common, or even his old friend Samuel, but Benson Cochran and his friends, Charlie and the fat one whose name he hadn't known, heroes of Saint Anthony's football team and all around bad boys.

His first kills.

Sometimes when he remembered those three, the boys who had made his life at Saint Anthony's so difficult, he wished he'd been more in control that night, more himself and less the animal. Whether to have been able to spare them, as Father Simon surely would have preferred, or to have experienced their deaths a little more fully he wasn't sure.

For some reason, that question disturbed him.

Far below, one of his little friends had caught a fish.

Jove dipped and within a few seconds was skimming the water himself, forcing his full attention on the rippling water in his path. If he caught something on his way north, he wouldn't have to wake up hungry again next twilight.

Kaine Moran was beginning to second-guess his decision to leave Connecticut. The change of scene had been exciting at first; from rural New England to what he'd always considered the coolest city in the world, the home of Starbucks Coffee and Grunge Metal: Seattle, Washington. He'd left the day after his eighteenth birthday, just over a year ago, and expected to have to struggle a little once he arrived, but a year - *a fucking year* – later and he still couldn't full time work as an artist.

If Seattle was such a happening place, why was the only full time work he could find on the docks or some crappy fast food joint? If it wasn't for his grandma he'd either be homeless of back in Moosup by now.

Seattle may or may not be the coolest city in the world, the jury was still out on that, but Vicky Moran was certainly the world's coolest grandma.

Kaine lived with Vicky in an old apartment building on California Street. Danforth Halls was a little shabby, but comfortable. Nothing fancy, but nice for the price.

She'd moved there a few years ahead of him to be closer to her brother-in-law, the last of his generation of the fecund Moran family. His Great Uncle Frank Moran – mostly known by his unlikely nickname Chuckles – was retired Navy, tall, straight-backed, crew cut and humorless. Uncle Chuckles had always been something of a boogeyman to the younger generation in the family whenever he graced them with his company at the yearly family reunion in Chicago. Grandma Vicky laughingly referred to Chicago as Ground Zero of the explosion of American Morans.

Vicky had grown up a lonely single child, and loved the living, breeding chaos that was the Moran family.

Thankfully, Kaine hadn't seen much of his Great Uncle Chuckles since moving in with his Grandma Vicky. Neither did Grandma Vicky, as far as he knew. They met once a month for coffee at the Starbucks on University Street. Kaine guessed this closer proximity to the late Donald Moran's brother hadn't done much to bring them closer.

She'd managed to find enough new interests to keep her occupied without his help though. She'd started out volunteering for Historic Seattle, and eventually found part-time work giving tours of Seattle's Underground through one of her HS connections. It supplemented her Social Security and the late Grandpa Moran's pension nicely.

She'd strictly forbidden Kaine from working fast food, and had only grudgingly allowed him to take part-time work on the docks.

"You didn't come all the way to Seattle to flip burgers,

Kaine," she said with uncharacteristic firmness. "You could have done that in Moosup."

Between his odd jobs on the dock and at the market, and the few freelance art gigs he'd managed to scrounge in the past few months, Kaine was at least able to help out a bit and have some pocket money.

The art jobs were too few and too far between to give him much hope, and mostly brainless commercial stuff, but it did beat flipping burgers.

While most of the stuff he did for money was digital, his favorite medium was still painting – real canvas, real paint, the outcome depending not on pre-plotted vectors and precise hexagonal hues, but the steadiness of his hand and the vision of his imagination. His personal work, the stuff he did just for himself, was flourishing. It seemed the city clicked with his creative dark side. His current favorite subject was the city itself – Seattle at night, a city of sinister lights and crooked towers, populated by monsters and demons.

The walls of his bedroom/studio were covered with his favorites. Others leaned against the walls, draped with dust cloths. He'd sent a few of these back to Moosup for his mom and pop. He thought his mom only liked them because they were his work, but his pop loved Kaine's dark vision of the city. It was the kind of shit that tweaked his own artistic fancy.

One of his not-so-dark Seattle cityscapes hung in the living room, across from a portrait he'd done of Grandma Vicky. She had taken photographs of them and emailed them to Uncle Chuckles, who had pronounced them *Not Bad*, high praise indeed.

He'd even had a promising, but ultimately fruitless

exchange with the proprietor of a contemporary/underground gallery, who thought his work showed promise, but didn't have the space for it.

But was Kaine the kind of guy who let repeated failure stop him? No, he constantly reminded himself, he was not.

It was in that spirit that he logged on to Craigslist for his daily search for freelance work, though without much enthusiasm. So it was something of a pleasant surprise when he found a response to a freelance job listing he'd replied to the day before.

He read, and his smile grew.

A winged monster terrorizing Seattle nightlife; this kind of shit was right up his alley.

Kaine had composed an email to the seeker of his professional artistic services, and was going over it a final time before sending it off when Grandma Vicky knocked on his door.

Kaine's finger hovered over the mouse for a moment, then shied away. He'd thought about asking Grandma Vicky if she'd ever heard of this Puget Devil, but didn't want to interrupt her morning routine, ablutions she called them. He didn't want to put off replying to the listing either. Sweet gigs don't hang around waiting for you while you scratched your ass. But she was out and about now, probably giving him a heads up on her plans for the day.

"Mornin' kiddo."

"Morning, Vicky." His Grandma Vicky was not fond of the G-word. "Heading out?"

Her eyes fell over his latest incomplete canvas and she gave a little nod. "Meeting Frankie at the Starbucks."

"Didn't you have coffee with Chuckles last week?"

She smiled. "I did, but he said he wanted to talk about something. Haven't heard him this frazzled since the time Donald told the story about when they were kids and the middle school principal caught Frankie urinating in his International's gas tank."

Kaine was stunned to momentary silence as he tried to ward off the image of a four-foot-tall Uncle Chuckles standing with his pants around his ankles, his ass in the breeze, and his pecker in a pickup's fuel port.

"You should come along," Grandma Vicky said. He's been asking about you. Wants to know how you're getting along."

"Wants to lecture me about pipe dreams and how a real man takes responsibility ... I think I'll pass." He felt bad enough living off Grandma Vicky to begin with, he didn't need Chuckles to make him feel worse.

She nodded again. "I'll pass along your best wishes then."

She winked at him, then turned to leave his room, and Kaine decided the email could wait another minute or two. Grandma Vicky, while not a native Seattleite, had been here a few years now. If she knew anything about The Puget Devil, it might be worth learning before he put his bid in for the job.

"Got a line on a freelance gig, photos or art for a national magazine." He paused for a second, wondering how to go on without making his potential freelance gig sound like a joke, and realized there was no way to do this.

"It's for American Star ... they're doing a series of pieces on something called The Puget Devil and I was ... what?"

Grandma Vicky had thrown her hands up to her face and started laughing.

"Oh, come one," Kaine flashed at her. "It's not The Metropolitan, but work is work."

Grandma Vicky shook her head and dropped her hands to her knees, bending down a little and leaning against his doorframe.

"It's not that," she managed to say through immoderate chuckles. "That's what Frankie wants to talk about. He was listening to his police scanner last night and heard something about a very large bird."

Coffee with Chuckles wasn't as bad as Kaine feared it would be. The subject of his current employment came up only once, and when Kaine told Chuckles he'd been commissioned to get a photo of The Puget Devil, old Chuckles had actually seemed interested.

Grandma Vicky, Kaine discovered, knew a bit about Seattle's newest urban legend, but Chuckles was a true fan. He followed The Puget Devil the way some fans follow their favorite wrestlers. He had police scanner audio, almost an hour total, copies of police reports, crime scene photos of alleged victims, and a few grainy surveillance camera photos.

A few friends in the police department, one an old

Navy buddy, had provided him with most of the pieces in his growing collection, and most of it was perfectly legal, not necessarily the kind of information the department wanted out, but still public information. Some of his stuff though, a few pieces from ongoing investigations, the nastier crime scene photos, were not public information.

When Kaine asked if he could look at the photos, Chuckles sat back in his seat and fixed appraising eyes on him.

"Oh, Kaine, why would you want to see stuff like that?" Grandma Vicky sounded utterly shocked.

"I understand your curiosity, boy." Chuckles drained half a fresh cup of espresso in one swallow and then set his cup down and leaned over the table toward Kaine. "Hell, I share it … but have you ever seen a dead body?"

Kaine wished he had something better to counter with, but had to admit he hadn't. "Not outside movies."

"And those aren't real. The pictures I have are real. They're not pretty, and once you see something like that you can't un-see it."

Grandma Vicky opted out of the conversation by turning in her chair to study Starbuck's selection of baked goods while she nursed her drink.

"They don't bother you though." Kaine thought he might be pushing him luck, tempting Uncle Chuckle's legendary anger, but he couldn't help it.

Chuckles was not angered, even managed a rare, if thin-lipped, smile. "Just a little bit. Thing is I've seen much worse, and not in photos."

He appeared on the edge off adding something else, then shook his head a little and downed the rest of his coffee. Kaine was almost sure he'd been about to add that he had in fact done worse, but held back out of consideration for Vicky.

Kaine was beginning to second guess all the horror stories he'd heard about Uncle Chuckles when he was younger. The man was certainly a bit on the chilly side, but seemed even tempered. Thinking about it, Kaine couldn't recall ever having seen his uncle's legendary temper in action. Maybe he'd learned to control it. Maybe the stories were exaggerations or outright lies spread by the relations he'd alienated during his life. There were plenty of those, Kaine knew, but he was actually beginning to like the man.

"I suppose, since it's work related …"

"Frankie, I wish you wouldn't …"

"He's not a kid, Victoria. It's his call."

Kaine considered Grandma Vicky's disapproving expression for a moment, then shook his head.

"Maybe not the ugly ones then. The surveillance photos and reports might help though.

Both Vicky and Chuckles nodded approval.

"I'll scan all the public records stuff for you … do you have a computer?"

Kaine was about to answer when Chuckles did something so unexpected it shocked him to silence. Chuckles chuckled.

"You're a modern young artist. Of course you have a computer."

Kaine and his Uncle Chuckles exchanged email addresses, and a half hour later, after he had regaled them both with the latest tales of The Puget Devil, left them to finish their drinks with a promise that he'd send everything he could Kaine's way by that afternoon.

"See," said Grandma Vicky, "He's not near as bad as everyone thinks."

Kaine agreed. Next time he had an invite to join Chuckles for coffee he might just take him up on it.

Uncle Chuckles was as good as his word. By six that evening Kaine received a series of emails with attached photos and documents, the last with a personal note that he might be able to arrange a couple of interviews if Kaine was interested.

Kaine was interested, and within a few hours he was speaking over the phone with a willing Puget Devil believer; a man who said he was only a believer because he'd actually seen the monster. Kaine didn't learn anything new from the short interview, but it reinforced the strategy he'd have to take if he was going to get the picture he needed.

This is insane, Kaine thought. *I'm planning this out like I actually believe this thing is real. That tabloid hack didn't take the stories seriously, or he would have asked for a photographer instead of a graphic artist.*

Well, Chuckles thought it was real, and Chuckles didn't strike Kaine as a pushover.

He realized then that he hadn't thought to ask his uncle why he was so convinced of the truth of this particular urban legend.

Kaine debated briefly, and decided it wasn't too late for one more call.

"Hello, Kaine." His uncle sounded amused rather than irritated by the lateness of the call.

"Hi uncle. Got us on caller ID?"

"Of course, but I didn't need to check it. I knew you'd call before the night was over."

Kaine was surprised into momentary silence. "How…?"

"There is one important question you neglected to ask me earlier." Chuckles chuckled again – Kaine still found that bizarre beyond his ability to express – and went on. "I was a little disappointed in you to be honest, but you seem like a smart kid, so I thought you'd get around to asking sooner rather than later."

Kaine smiled. What a weird day. "Asking what?"

"Why a hard-headed old fart like me buys so deeply into such a kooky urban legend."

Kaine laughed. "Yeah, that's pretty much it."

"Easiest answer in the world." Kaine thought he could hear a smile in the old man's voice. "I saw it."

Kaine accepted this strain on his credulity, and after a moment's pause, asked the next logical question.

"Where did you se it?"

"In the old underground."

"I thought," Kaine said, trying to keep any skepticism out of his voice, "that the old underground was closed off."

"It is, mostly, but if someone is cold enough, or desperate enough to find a place to sleep, they can find a way in. Many do."

Kaine waited for his uncle to elaborate, but there was only silence on his uncle's end.

"Why were you down there?"

"This … this is between you and I, no one else is to know about this. Not even Vicky."

"Okay."

"I have a few friends who live down there. I don't go down to catch up, no good old days talk, they wouldn't like it. It would shame them. But I leave stuff where they can find it. Food and blankets. I got lost one night, didn't find my way out until after dark, and I ran right into it."

There were a few more moments of silence between them that Kaine had no idea how to fill. Then his uncle spoke again.

"Whatever you may think, it is real, and whatever people on the streets are saying, it is not a mindless killer. It could have killed me ... would have been the easiest thing in the world for it ... but it didn't. It let me go. But I wouldn't want to press my luck by getting caught down there with it again, and I wouldn't recommend you do that either, so you'll need a new camera with a good telescopic lens."

Kaine was already thinking the same thing.

———

The next night Kaine was ready with a new telescopic attachment on his uncle's only slightly used 35mm digital Canon. His vantage point was not the best, he had to aim up to target the roof above the Needle's observation deck, and he would have much preferred a straight on view, but he supposed that was a problem when trying to photograph one of the tallest structures in the city. He'd found a relatively secluded spot just off Broad Street and sat behind the wheel of his Grandma Vicky's car as the sun set and full dark finally descended on the city.

He was prepared for a long and very likely fruitless night. As it turned out, he didn't have to wait long at all.

Kaine got his pictures, and any remaining doubts he had in his uncle's crazy stories about The Puget Devil were swept away.

Charles liked cactuses. He didn't know why, he just did. He liked tall saguaro with their spindly arms cocked to the sky. He liked tiny flowering echinopsis with their short-lived but fragrant blooms, and the fragile cholla, which drew the eyes to its unexpected beauty. His favorites were Christmas Cactuses, the lovely echlumbergera, with their blood red blooms.

He kept a small one potted on his dashboard, and thought he'd like to take a little time while they were passing through Colorado to dig up a few new ones. They were almost to the not-quite city of Canyon, would be there shortly, and he needed to stop for a few essentials anyway. Maybe they could make a detour into the boonies to pick up something new for his collection.

On his list of favorite things, cactuses was number fourteen or fifteen, a few spots above the *Name That Sound* bit he and Crow used to do on their radio show, and a few below getting nice and mellow with a bowl of Nepalese hash. Second on his list was his boots. He'd take those fuckers to the grave, just like their last owner.

Charles's fourth favorite thing, the thing he was currently concerned with, was his porn collection. It was sorely outdated. He was at least three months behind on all his favorites, having spent a little more time than they'd expected on the other side of the big nowhere.

Not that it wasn't good to be back home for a more extended visit, but Charles always thought of *home* as a fluid concept ... where the heart was and all that crap. At that moment home happened to be the large and comfortable cab of their travelin' van, and home was sorely lacking a few of the more basic comforts. Any form of basic intoxication, for instance, or an up to date Penthouse.

And maybe, if the boss was in a persuadable mood, he'd take a tour of that haunted prison he'd read about.

"Pit stop," Charles shouted, thumping the dividing wall between the cab and cargo area. He'd spotted a mini-mall with a convenience store, liquor store, and video store, a bit of one stop shop paradise right there in Colorado.

"Do you have a list or are you just winging it?"

Charles rolled his eyes. "Are you fucking kidding me?"

There was a loud clicking from behind the closed partition. "The last time I sent you in without a list we spent a week eating kippers and Spam."

"I had a craving," Charles explained. "Remember that time you made me get you ten large buckets of KFC? I was shiting drumsticks for a week."

Charles thought about concluding with his own personal opinion that watching a giant bird-man chow down on a small army of his dismembered, breaded, and deep-fried cousins was repulsive, but decided to spare his friend's feelings.

Andy laughed, pushed open the partition and poked his head out far enough to face Charles. "Fried chicken is not kippers, and I had a good excuse."

"You were stoned. You had the munchies."

"Five minutes," Andy said. "Just hold your water."

Five minutes later, give or take, Charles was packing a basket through the isle of a filthy little market looking for canned veggies.

He found them, swept random cans onto the basket, made a mark through *canned peas*. He hadn't paid any particular attention to the cans he'd tumbled in, but thought the chances were good at least one of them contained peas. Next came bread, then mayo, cheese and lunchmeat. He dropped in a package of Olive Loaf, which he'd always thought looked like processed vomit, then added two cans of bacon flavored Spam.

Yum.

When he'd cleared the list he added a few things for himself, then lugged the heavily laden basket to the counter. The cashier was a beefy woman with a lot of facial hair and tiny little eyes mostly obscured by swags of hanging flesh topped by a bushy unibrow. He briefly considered saving some cash with a few head games, and decided it wasn't the time or place. Some folks came around quicker than others, and Charles had been making an honest effort to stay out of trouble lately.

He was digging through the deep pockets of his duster

when he spotted the latest issue of American Star on the news rack.

American Star was not on his short list of essential reading material, though the Weeping Jesus Taco Chip story had made him laugh until he puked, but the cover of this issue caught his eye in a special way. He looked at the photo, then re-read the headline and did a quick bit of mental arithmetic. The answer he arrived at startled him out of his relentlessly buoyant mood. He pulled two copies from the rack and slapped them down on the counter.

The corpulent cashier regarded him with irritation.

"It's all bull-shit you know. Don't know why you'd waste money on it."

"Absolute bullshit," Charles agreed, and when she only continued to stare at him added, "Utter crapolla."

When she still made no move to ring them up he added a heart felt "piss off," just to impress upon her that while he was in complete agreement with her, he was also in a bit of a rush.

"Moron," she concluded, and with the conversation at an obvious end, finished ringing him up and sent him on his way.

Charles paused outside the doors, letting the sunlight hit his face in a very agreeable way. He basked in it, like a lizard on a rock.

"Dude!"

Charles turned to find a rather filthy man sitting on the newspaper dispenser next to an ashtray, picking through it for salvageable butts. His eyes were sunken and bloodshot, his face a riot of scraggly beard and dirt, his cracked lips ringed with sores.

"Wicked dreads," the man said, his face breaking into a sunny, and Charles thought hopeful, grin.

His mood partially restored by the warmth of the sun on his face, Charles dipped into a deep bow, one of his long dreadlocks stirring to life long enough to doff his hat at the bum then pull it back over his head.

The man goggled satisfactorily at Charles for a second before clumsily catching a quarter that seemed to have leapt out from under Charles's cap to spin, glittering in the sunlight, toward his open hand.

A few seconds later the quarter became a large roach, which skittered around the bum's hand and bit him before leaping free and vanishing beneath the newspaper dispenser.

The bum screamed.

Charles smiled, his good mood now fully restored. He enjoyed nothing more than throwing a good mind-fuck. After a quick bombing run at the liquor store, he walked to the van to show Andy that week's American Star headline story.

Andy Crow was not happy. He was a cowboy without a horse, a predator without prey, a bounty hunter with no bounty, and the side gigs were getting a bit old, losing their sense of fun. The radio show had simply been more trouble than it was worth; a great lure for the scum of this particular earth, people this world seemed happy enough to be rid of and his employers were happy enough to use, but a logistical nightmare.

The phony porn shoots were more pleasure than business, but willing participants were tough to come by outside of Los Angeles, where every other woman thought she was the next Angelina Jolie and had no problems beginning their careers at the bottom, so to speak.

He thought he'd gotten used to being an exile, but he found himself missing his homeland more than ever. Home was out of the question, but he thought he could at least settle for a place where he wouldn't have to hide.

Charles, always cheerful, a cup half full kind of guy, told him time and again that all he needed was something to occupy him. A new bounty would have been his preference, something challenging, an involved job with a nice payoff. There weren't any bounties on this side of what Charles liked to call *The Big Nowhere*, so they were headed back to Sunny LA to make some work.

He was thinking maybe he'd have Charles use his magnificent powers of persuasion to start a cult - a birdman cult. He could set himself up as a godhead and Charles a messiah, have lots of filthy sex with the more attractive members, promising to take them to a new world as a final reward for faithful service, then, and this was the best part, actually take them to a new world when he got sick of them. It was an idea Charles pitched every now and then, and which Andy was beginning to consider ever more seriously.

Andy could feel his mood lifting a bit just thinking about it.

He decided to have Charles make a little side trip into the high desert after they left town. Charles had mentioned the abundance of cacti in the area, and it would make his day to be able to scrounge around the hills and pick up a few before moving on. The cactus fetish was just one of the many strange things Andy didn't get about his friend, but like all the others, he took it in stride. He'd put up with a lot for Charles's continued company.

The man was just fun to be around.

What was the point of living if you can't have a little fun?

"Boss! Got something here you're gonna wanna see!"

Andy stirred in his office recliner. Something in Charles's voice was different, and it took Andy a moment to recognize it. He was worried about something. The man who thrived on trouble, whose preferred drug was adrenalin, was uneasy about something.

Inversely, Andy felt the first pang of anticipation, the prelude to actual excitement. This was a feeling so unfamiliar these days he paused to enjoy it for a moment before responding.

"Yo, Andy!"

Charles's voice sounded muffled, as if passing through a thick wall, but the door between Andy's office and the van's cargo area was wide open. The opening between here and there was a funny thing, and sometimes temperamental. It did funny things to sound, softened it somehow, and looking through it was like looking through the side of a giant fishbowl. A fishbowl made of gelatin. It also tickled like hell when you walked through it, a sensation that Charles called Quantum Shivers. It made him giggle every time, and when Charles got the giggles, Andy always caught them like a cold. He didn't know if it was Charles's unusual persuasive talent getting away from him, or just the fact that he found his good vibes infectious. Maybe they amounted to the same thing. It didn't matter. Andy just accepted it as a part of life with Mr. Greene.

"Is the van safe?"

"For a while," Charles said.

"Then lock it up and step on in."

Charles stepped through the door a moment later, and Andy settled back into his Lazy Boy to wait out his predictable fit of the giggles. They came and went rapidly, a sure sign that something serious was nagging at him.

"What's on your mind?". Andy gestured to the plush leather sofa against the adjacent wall. "Relax man, you're getting twitchy."

Charles shot Andy a furtive glance, then watched his boots. "This is gonna blow your fuckin' mind man."

His strangely long legs kicked the tail of his duster out behind him as he strode across the high domed office, a cavern lit by the steady glow of what appeared to be a million shining crystals hanging from the ceiling.

Once the shock of the room's strangeness wore off a bit and you grew used to the brightness, the million *crystals* resolved themselves into a network of hanging icicle Christmas lights. The cavern's lights were operated by Clapper and powered by a massive magnetic power generator tucked away in a lower cavern.

Beside Andy's recliner was a desk, Charles's desk since Andy was too tall and awkwardly built to use it comfortably, and a newish laptop computer.

The van was equipped with satellite Internet and a wireless router, powered by the van's more conventional battery, but it didn't actually work unless you left the door between the cave and van open.

Most of their old radio equipment was gone, sold off a piece at a time on the road, but what was left hunkered in a far and dark corner of the cavern under large canvases.

The office, the largest cavern in the complex Andrew Crow and Charles Greene called home, was as wide open as an empty cathedral and large enough for Andy to stretch his wings and flap about when the mood took him. It was Andy, with Charles watching in a fit of laughter, who hung the Christmas lights from the high ceiling.

You look like a hummingbird, he'd shouted, rocking with laughter until Andy swooped down on him and hoisted him into the air by an ankle.

Charles spun and plopped down into the overstuffed leather sofa, shifting his weight into it until his backside was comfortably cocooned. He dropped the plastic convenience store bag between his feet, pulled out his rolled-up copies of The American Star, and tossed one to Andy.

Andy, his reflexes always lightning quick, was out of his chair almost too fast for Charles to track, standing halfway between his La-Z-Boy and the sofa, the magazine in his clawed hand.

"Boss," Charles said, holding his own copy out so Andy could read the bold printed headline, "You need to read this."

Andy read the story in his La-Z-Boy with his feet kicked up and a bottle of Tap & Die Malt Liquor in his free hand. Tap & Die was a hard to find micro-brew that Andy had dragged them around the State of New York twice to find, and the supply was limited. Andy only allowed himself one a week.

When he was finished, he turned back to the front and looked at the photo of The Puget Devil again before rolling it up and dropping it to the floor.

"This could be trouble, Andy. This is the kind of shit that gets noticed." A dreadlock slipped from Charles's cap like a snake, slithered across his cheek and planted a bomber joint between his waiting lips. A second followed with a disposable Bic and lit him up.

Andy nodded once, slowly.

"Tell me what you're thinking, old friend."

Andy was already there, but he wanted to hear Charles confirm it. Charles had always called Andy Boss, but it was an affectation. Andy was not his boss. They were partners, had been since the bad old days, and Andy valued his opinions. The guy was sharp, but he was also creative, and creative problem solving was a skill Andy valued.

"There's only two ways to go with this. We have to shut him down or bring him in. Dead or under our control, we have to make The Puget Devil disappear."

"And which of the two would you prefer?" Andy was honestly curious. It was a question of great importance, the answer to which he needed to hear before they could proceed, as they always had, equal partners in this new venture. He wanted Charles's honest answer, not what Charles's thought he wanted to hear.

Charles grinned, that wide and daffy grin that bloomed like a shark's from his pudgy face. Another of his living dreadlocks slithered from beneath his cap and held out something.

Andy leaned forward, dropping his chair's footrest to plant his feet on the cavern floor, and focused his razor keen vision on the object.

Not a fat joint this time, but a cigar with a blue ribbon crisscrossed beneath its cellophane wrapper.

It's A Boy!

"I think it's time to celebrate, my old friend. You're a papa!" He stripped the cellophane from the cigar and planted it in the corner of his wide mouth not occupied by his joint. Somehow, he still had enough mouth left over to talk. "And since I know you don't smoke, I'll smoke it for you."

That was what Andy wanted to hear.

Andy kicked his feet up again and poured the rest of the Tap & Die down his throat. He clicked his beak in pleasure, then hurled the bottle to the high ceiling. It smashed, raining amber glass pebbles down on them.

"More stuff in the cab," Charles said, butting his joint out on the floor when it was smoked down to a barely manageable nub. "Be right back."

Andy closed his eyes, laying back in his recliner, and folded his hands across his chest. Certain key phrases from the Star story recurred to him – *gruesome attacks, mounting death toll, vicious monster.* He had never even met the boy, and he was already proud of him.

"Leave the door open," Andy called to Charles's retreating flap of coat. "I want to use the computer."

Andy leaned toward the desk and scooped the laptop onto his lap, a place one would logically expected it to spend a lot of time, though it somehow didn't, and opened the web browser.

He had a little investigating of his own to do before kicking off, and The American Star website was as good a place as any to start.

It was Strip Night for Doug, his favorite of all nights, and he was spending the first bit of it in The Mirage Hotel's Jet Club. Music, drinks, dancing (though not for him – Doug hadn't danced since his disastrous High School prom), and possible celebrity shenanigans he could write about later.

A memorable night at The Jet Club a few years back had been his inspiration for *The Adventures of an All American Lesbian*, so he regarded the place as something of a lucky charm. It was also a great place to meet up with hookers.

The Jet Club was not a place where hookers trolled for johns, like most twenty-first century Vegas establishments The Jet Club was a mostly prostitute free zone, but Doug always met his escorts at public places, and The Jet Club was ideal. Wide open enough to spot his lady when she went to the bar, busy enough to sneak out if he didn't like what he saw.

Vegas had almost as many hookers as tourists, but

finding them had become a bit of a challenge since the city had gone *Family Friendly*. Modern practitioners of the world's oldest profession in Sin City had either moved onto some of the less savory streets, places where Doug wouldn't be caught dead, or had started advertising their services in local publications and fliers as bachelor's guides, escorts, and models.

These ladies were safer, and less likely to give you something pleasant like cock warts or syphilis, but scams still flourished. Someone who made a habit of giving their addresses out to escort services would, sooner or later, end up robbed, burgled, or shot. Doug always met with them publicly, and always somewhere where he could watch them from a safe distance, long enough to get a vibe. He didn't know if his vibes were accurate, but he went with them. Sometimes he got a bad vibe about a woman and simply migrated to another hotel bar to call someone else out. A few times he'd spotted women speaking with possible accomplices, usually men, who might turn up later in the evening to cause trouble for him.

Mostly they seemed okay.

He'd never been robbed, blackmailed, or victimized in any way, so Doug stuck to his ritual.

Tonight, he was meeting Lisa, a skinny little thing with melon-sized tits and reddish-blonde hair that fell in waves past her ass. At least that was what the photos on her advert showed. False advertisement sucked, but it happened.

His boss, the sour old fuck, had a saying that Doug liked. *If people can lie, they usually will.*

If the real-life Lisa was anything like the photos in her advert, he was in for a hell of a night.

Doug liked long hair, fucking loved it. He liked to run his hands through it, to wind it through his fists like reins when he mounted them from behind. One hooker, a freaky little Native American thing with hair down to her ankles, and no hair anywhere else on her body, had charged him an extra Grant for the chance to choke her with her own braids. Doug never really had a taste for S&M, but hell, you should try everything at least once.

***

There were no celebrity shenanigans at The Jet Club that night, which was okay. Sometimes you just wanted to forget work and relax.

Lisa showed up at a quarter to nine wearing a form fitting red dress, opened to show as much breast as legally possible. Heads following her as she walked to the bar and leaned over it to talk to the bartender. She had his attention at once. One second he was in deep conversation with a funky little brunette with spiked hair and a rag of a shirt that barely covered a pair of little boiled-egg tittles, then he was in front of Lisa, nodding at her, his mouth hanging open and his lust on full display.

Behold ... the power of cleavage.

Doug had already paid for her first drink, which the bartender was now pouring her without asking for ID. She looked like a ripe sixteen or seventeen. Probably just good genetics and a liberal application of makeup, but they were supposed to check.

Lisa slid onto a stool and turned slowly, searching the

bar. Her eyes fell over him, just for a moment, and Doug thought she gave him a knowing smile before turning to take her drink.

The bartender stayed to chat her up, ignoring orders from all around and an indignant parting caw from the funky little brunette.

Doug watched her for another minute as she shooed the bartender away and nursed her drink, thinking there was something a little strange about her, not being able to place it. Then the other men began to move in, flanking her, offering drinks, money, their very souls for all he knew, and Doug decided he'd better seal the deal before she got tired of waiting and took another offer.

Doug finished his rum and coke and rose from his table to meet her. The upper floor of the bar was crowded, he had to weave through chaotic flows of foot traffic and dodge around clusters of patrons too high on life, and maybe a little Ecstasy, to actually sit. The large dance floor was mostly deserted, but the extra space seemed to give the few dancers using it license to shake their sweating booties with extra vigor, and Doug had to keep his eyes on them as a couple came dangerously close to starting an unwanted threesome with him. By eleven o'clock the dancers crammed onto and around the floor would be so thick the collective body heat would threaten to raise the temperature of Las Vegas Boulevard.

Lisa watched him, her eyes darting occasionally to the men clustering around her, her mouth forming unheard responses to them.

As Doug approached, her admirers followed her gaze toward him, their postures changing almost immediately from easygoing hipster slouch to straight-backed aggression.

Doug smiled, he couldn't help it.

"Lisa," he said, taking her offered hand in his and leading her away from the bar.

"Doug," she let him lead her to a quieter patch of floor near the gaming machines. "I thought you were going to stand me up."

Lisa's hand slipped from his and slid up his arm, her fingernails, the same garish red as her dress, gliding through the coarse and curly black arm hair, teasing up gooseflesh.

"Would you like to sit?" Doug could have just dragged her straight up to his rented room, she was a sure thing after all, no need to waste finesse on her, but sure thing or not, it never hurt to be a gentleman.

Lisa stared into his eyes for a moment, her lips curving into a sexy smirk, then nodded. She held the drink in her free hand, "It would be rude not to finish this."

"I've never been in here before," Lisa admitted when they were seated near the Jet Club's dedicated gamers. She looked around, taking in the central dance floor, already beginning to fill up, and smiled. Not the sly sexy smile this time, but real and unaffected. "I like the lighting."

"You're not from around here, are you?" Doug didn't give a shit where she was from or where she was going once he was finished with her, but he had the gentleman rule.

Lisa didn't answer, but she gave him a look over the top of her glass, a kind of bland, impatient look.

She finished her drink in a swallow and placed her

empty glass to the side, then reached for his hand. "It's getting crowded. Do you have a place for us to go?"

Right down to business.

Doug could appreciate that.

Doug had reserved the cheapest room The Mirage had available, a King Deluxe, but even cheap rooms at The Mirage were nice. The king bed was close to the room's window. The view of Vegas was postcard perfect, a circus of light, an improbable magic city sprouted from the desert.

Doug lay naked on the center of the large bed, the sheets pulled up to his waist, hands cupped beneath his head, watching the rising moon, just past full, against the backdrop of sky that would have been starlit if not for the city's light pollution.

Doug was okay with that. He'd take neon light over star light. The stars had always made him feel too small.

Something unidentifiable, a darker shape against the deepening midnight blue of the desert sky, shot past, casting its shadow for the tiniest instant.

Doug blinked, then smiled.

Big fucking bird!

Lisa was in the bathroom freshening up for the evening. He could just hear her voice over the sound of running water, high and sweet, singing what could have been an old folk tune, the kind that had been popular in the psychedelic sixties and still was to a dwindling hard core of hippies, the few who hadn't succumbed to yuppie-hood. Maybe it was some goofy new age mantra. She certainly seemed the type, not exactly a burnout, but a little off.

With a body like that she could get away with being a little off. Who was going to complain?

Doug was beginning to lose interest in the moon or whatever big fucking birds might be flapping around outside. He was about to call for her, he was a paying customer after all, when the running water stopped.

Her song, or mantra, of whatever the hell it was, tapered off, and Doug saw the bar of light coming from under the bathroom door wink out.

The door opened, and Lisa stepped out.

She was a shape in the darkness, flesh washed by neon light, landscaped by shadow.

"Are you ready for this?"

Stunned into silence, nearly hypnotized by her perfection, Doug watched her approach. He answered her, not knowing what he'd meant to say until it was said.

"Yes … I love you!"

What the blue fuck is this?

He didn't know where that had come from. He recoiled back into his stacked pillows, closed his eyes and shook his head. He felt like he was stoned … drugged, but he didn't know how she could have drugged him. He'd finished his last drink of the night before he'd met her. Unless … there was the bartender … but no, that was just paranoid thinking.

"Doug, look at me."

He did, and felt all doubt, all questions, pushed aside by a swell of lust; lust like a stroke of lightning, and a roaring need that pounded in his chest like thunder. He felt full of electricity, an overcharged battery ready to explode.

"Now," he said. "Don't make me wait!"

He loved her. He wanted her more than he had ever wanted a woman. He would do anything for her. He wished she would command him to perform something pointlessly reckless, perilously dangerous, something criminal, so he could prove his devotion to her.

But more than that, he wanted to get inside her. His erection felt like a stick of dynamite in his hand, hard and unstable, its fuse lit. He didn't want to explode in his hand, he wanted to explode inside of her. After that, he could fade away and die.

Something's wrong here.

Yes, he supposed there was. She'd done something to him.

He didn't really care anymore.

Lisa took another step toward him, still across the room, and then was crawling across the bed, her back arched and limbs taut, like a cheetah stalking its prey. He hadn't blinked, hadn't taken his eyes off her, didn't see how she could have crossed the room to him in a single step, but she was pulling the sheets off him, and he didn't care how she had gotten there. She was there. That was all that mattered.

Lisa regarded his penis with something like hunger, and in a quick, fluid motion slid herself over him, and poised herself over it.

She grabbed him by his cheeks … damn, she had a strong grip … and lowered her face to his.

"You are really going to enjoy this," she assured him.

Yes, he knew he would.

And he did. Right up until the end.

Doug couldn't say how long it had lasted, time seemed to have slipped past him in a rush while he lay beneath her. He'd thought he would finish quickly, but somehow he didn't. She brought him to the edge, and seemed to hold him there forever, bringing him to a level of pleasure that bordered on torture.

It went on, and he thought his heart would explode in his chest, and after an undeterminable time he wanted it to end. He wanted to finish, but couldn't, and when he tried to push her away, tried to pull himself from her intimate grip, he couldn't. She was strong. She held him down with one hand, caressed him with the other. Her privates held him fast, gripped him like a Chinese finger trap. The harder he fought to get away, the tighter she gripped him.

She laughed at him.

"Just another man," she said. "You think your rod is mighty, but it's only a needy little piece of meat."

"Please," Doug panted, out of breath. "No more."

"You're the boss," she said, and winked at him.

She bared her teeth at him in a grimace and plunged down onto him, sinking him deeper into her than he had ever gone into a woman. He felt as if their genitals had melted together, merged into a single hermaphroditic organ, and incredibly, he felt himself pulled deeper still, as if she'd tear it right off.

Then is was over. He closed his eyes and grabbed the sheets beneath him as a rush that felt less like a squirt and more like a hot wave blasted out of him and into her. It felt as if she was taking more than his seed. It felt like she was draining his very life.

"You're a good boy, Dougy," and her voice was different, but familiar. Very familiar.

Doug opened his eyes. The color drained out of his face, and his mouth fell open in a silent, breathless scream.

He couldn't breathe. He felt his heartbeat racing faster, faster, knew his pump would soon seize up or explode in his chest, and again wished it would.

The young and perfect body poised above him was gone. The creature riding him was old, wrinkled, dead.

His mother.

Then he fell out of her, shriveled out of her, felt himself going numb.

In the instant before the darkness swallowed him, he heard another voice.

"Easy girl. I didn't say you could kill him."

The voice, high pitched and reedy, somehow not human, laughed.

Doug awoke in the dark and felt a tentative kind of relief, the shaky relief of the dreamer on waking. Now he only needed light to burn away the last of the nightmare.

And just what the hell had she been, anyway? A succubus?

Clearly, he'd been reading too much of his own work.

After a few groggy waking moments, Doug's tentative relief evaporated. He was not laying down in his own bed, or even a reasonably comfy hotel bed. He was seated on a hard chair, his ankles bound to the thick legs, his wrists tied together behind his seat's flat wooden back.

The thing he'd always feared most about his weekly forays on The Strip had finally happened.

Kidnapped.

What had the bitch given him to knock him out? Something powerful. Something hallucinogenic.

Whatever it was, it had left him with a wicked headache.

So, what the hell do I do now?

Fuck it, only one thing to do.

"Hey!" Doug flinched back against his seat with the force of the unexpected echo, then dropping his volume, continued. "Someone feel like explaining this to me?"

Very distantly, came a reply.

"Hey, Andy, I think you've got some 'splaining to do."

An echoing approach, the sound of large feet grinding gravel, then a sound like tarp blowing in the wind. A flapping. As it drew closer, Doug became surer it was coming from above.

He strained back in his seat to scan overhead, but the darkness above him was as solid as the darkness around him.

"What the hell's going on?" The flapping sound, more like giant wings than a flapping tarp now, he thought, stopped, and small rocks rained down around him.

When Andy spoke, Doug screamed in surprise. The unseen man sounded bare inches away now.

"Doug Oleander, AKA Ty Scott. I'm a big fan of your writing." It was the strange voice from the end of his horrible hallucinogenic dream, if it was a dream. "I just wanted a change to meet with you and talk about your work."

For a moment Doug was incapable of coherent

thought, let alone speech. Doug knew he had crazy readers, but crazy fans? He was a tabloid writer for fuck's sake, not a rock star.

And then the answer hit him. Religious nuts, very likely mightily offended by his *Weeping Jesus Taco Chip* story.

"I bet he'd be a lot more agreeable to your interview if we turned the lights on for him." This voice was warm, even jolly, James Earl Jones on the edge of hysterical giggles. "The dark really freaks some people out."

Andy grunted ascent. "Sure, why the hell not. No need to make our friend any more uncomfortable than absolutely necessary."

A few tense moments passed in silence, then overhead, far overhead, a trio of floodlights stabbed down at Doug. He cried out as the sudden brightness burned his eyes.

He was at the bottom of a deep shaft, fifty feet or more, and a pudgy, grinning face hovered over the edge above. Long black dreadlocks twisted around the man's face.

Then Doug faced forward again, and saw ...

Very tall, very nearly naked, he wore only a pair of large cargo shorts. His body was jet black and shiny. Feathered. He hung upside down, his long taloned toes gripping the stony shaft wall. His wings, massive things that would nearly fill the shaft wall to wall fully spread, opened slightly and beat the air before folding against his back again. The face, hanging upside down a few feet from Doug's, was narrow, sleek, and beaked. The eyes were like polished obsidian.

Andy held the latest issue of The American Star out to Doug, the cover clearly visible.

The Puget Devil, what the photographer claimed was a completely unaltered shot, rising from Seattle's monorail tunnel.

"I'm very curious about this chap here. I want you to tell me everything you know about him."

"Fair warning," the jolly voice from above cut in. "Andy usually gets what he wants, so just spill it all and save yourself a lot of hassle."

After a brief hysterical interlude Doug regained as much of his composure as he was ever likely to have again and spilled his guts.

CHAPTER 7

Jove became aware of his personal photographer by chance alone, scavenging papers from trashcans after dawn to kindle fires in his den. He had seen a few mentions of *Something Strange in Seattle* in the local papers, but it was a news magazine where he saw his picture. It was him, very clearly him, taking flight from the observation deck atop the Space Needle. The bold black headline read *Puget Devil ... Winged Monster Terrorizes Seattle.*

He stuck the rolled-up bundle of loose newspaper under his arm then shook The American Star open, shuffling through the pages until he found himself again, this time a more distant silhouette against a full moon so large and low in the sky it appeared to be floating in the Pacific.

Winged Monster ...

With a stealthy glance around to see who else was out in the streets with him – almost no one it turned out - Jove rolled The American Star up and shoved it under his arm with the other papers.

Someone was following him, watching him, and he hadn't sensed it. The beast inside, deep inside with the first rays of morning sun shining down on him, grumbled, and Jove understood it to be an admonition, a stern scolding from his subconscious.

See what happens when you try to tame me?

Jove ran barefoot down the sidewalk through the dawn's light toward the alley that connected, albeit in a very roundabout way, to his part of the underground, where he could hide from the city's daytime hoards and read about himself in The American Star in safety and privacy.

But not for too long. He was dead tired. He'd traveled all over the city the night before, all over the sound, and had eaten well, and he was dead tired.

Back in place, the underground room with a nest of old blankets to sleep in and his few personal possessions, Jove lit a cautious fire in a ring of old bricks and read by the flickering light. At first, settling comfortably into his rough bed and opening the magazine to his story, he was nervous. He knew this was the kind of magazine that made up a lot of crazy and outrageous stuff that no one believed in, but what if they knew about him … really knew, and someone *was* following him, taking pictures from a distance.

Did they know what the Puget Devil became at dawn?

He didn't know how anybody could, but he was still scared.

Once he started reading his fear eased. The pictures were real, were him, but the story itself was nothing but hearsay, some guesswork, and a lot of outright lies.

By the time he finished with the story, what he now understood to be just one of a series of them, he had forgotten about being tired. He was angry, angrier than he'd been since the day everything had gone so wrong back at Saint Anthony's. Words and phrases, kept recurring to him even after he'd shut the hateful thing and thrown it into a far, dark corner of his room.

Monster ... hunts the innocent and helpless ... inhuman freak ... killer ... a demon risen from hell, Satan's first lone warrior in an upcoming end of days war.

And something about Jesus on a taco chip?

Bless me Father, for I have sinned. It has been a week since my last confession.

What have you to confess today, my son?

I think I'm turning into a demon.

Those words, that confessional, recurred to him with bitter clarity, and a superstitious fear squeezed him. It was reflexive, he knew. His years of religious training had conditioned him to fear God. His disbelief in that *Big Guy in the Sky* wasn't a cure for the conditioned fear.

Jove settled back into his bed and closed his eyes, using the same force of will he's used to tame his monster to calm his swelling indignation and rage. The fear would have to fade on its own. He couldn't do anything about that.

He could see a dancing redness, the flames moving to their own secret and chaotic rhythm, through his closed eyelids. The red glow faded by slow degrees, and when it finally faded to pure black, he couldn't tell if it was just darkness, or sleep had finally taken him. He didn't care much one way or the other. The darkness was a comfort, and if it was sleep, then it was dreamless, which was also something of a blessing.

———

Kaine's excitement about finally finding steady work, not in art, but photography, which was still cool, began to wane when he read the first Puget Devil story. When he read the third installment, the second with his accompanying photographs, he began to actively dislike his employer. He realized he should have expected it, The American Star was not noted for its journalistic integrity, but Ty Scott had taken all of the collected information Kaine had sent with the pictures and wiped his creative ass with them.

All the collected evidence, if you could call it that, suggested a strange but benign, or at least neutral, being that sailed the night skies of The Emerald City, and Ty had turned it into a bloodthirsty monster, attacking and killing old women and babies on a nightly basis.

"You have a highly developed sense of fair play," Vicky said. "I thought your generation was supposed to be aloof and amoral."

Uncle Chuckles, sitting next to Vicky across from Kaine sipped his coffee, then shook his head.

"Naw, the young have always been the watchmen of the highest moral standards that old bastards like me have mostly abandoned."

The monthly Starbucks visit had become weekly now, and Kaine always accompanied them. His father found Kaine's new affinity to the dreaded Uncle Chuckles hilarious.

A crowd of teenagers pushed in, swaggering past Kaine's table on their way to order their frappuccino and lattes. Chuckles frowned at the passing heads of dyed black hair and skinny jeans that failed to fully cover a single backside.

"Unfortunately, they get a little creepier every year." Chuckles concluded, taking solace from the modern youth in his coffee again.

"I remember when greasers and beatniks used to make him glow with rage." Grandma Vicky laughed. "I think he misses them now."

Chuckles grunted something that might have been assent. "Those Goths are just weird."

"Oh, I don't think they're called Goths anymore. They're called Elmo now, like the little red guy on Sesame Street."

Kaine opened his mouth to say, *emo, they're called emo now*. What came out instead was "I think I'm going to quit."

Having finally spit it out, he waited in a nervous kind of anticipation for his uncle's reaction. He knew Vicky would be okay with any decision he made, but he didn't want to lose Chuckle's newly gained respect. Didn't want to come across as a whiner or quitter.

"That's your call son." Chuckles paused for a moment, seemed to consider his next words, then shrugged and went on. "I happen to agree with you about that rag and its writers. It's the worst kind of journalism ... barely disguised fiction."

Kaine nodded. "Yeah, but this is different. This time it's real."

Chuckles nodded. "It's up to you to decide if it's a fight you want to pick."

"What?" Kaine was about to add *it's the truth*, when Vicky cut in.

"Most people know those magazines are nonsense, cheap entertainment. True or not, no one really believes it. Your photos are good, but no one is going to think they're real, so does it matter if the story is a lie?"

"You," Chuckles said, fixing a stern gaze on Vicky over the lip of his cup, "are one cynical old woman."

Vicky threw a balled up straw wrapper at Chuckles. It bounced off his forehead and he flinched back, slopping coffee onto the table.

"Watch your mouth, you old curmudgeon."

Together, they began to laugh.

Kaine exchanged a quick look with one of the emo kids. The boy dropped his expression of world weary disinterest, his cultivated contempt for all things status quo, for a moment to smile and shake his head.

Crazy old people.

Kaine grinned back, then turned his attention back to his crazy old people. His favorite people.

Vicky changed the subject, recounting her latest adventures in the world of The Historical Society, and Chuckles told them about an upcoming trip to San Francisco for a memorial service. An old war buddy, one of Vietnam's reluctant soldiers, had passed, and Chuckles was traveling to his least favorite city in the world to pay his respects.

Kaine sat silent for the rest of the visit, half listening, considering. Wondering if the Puget Devil, who he had to admit no sane person would believe in unless they saw it, him, her, whatever the hell it was, for themselves, was worth losing a paying job over.

By the time they parted ways, Chuckles for home, Vicky off to her shift at the Underground Tour, Kaine for wherever he felt like drifting off to, he decided not to decide, at least not right away. For now, he'd take his pictures and wait. Build up his professional portfolio, and maybe write his own piece on The Puget Devil.

Jove spent the night ignoring his hunger and suppressing the urge to fly, something he could not have made himself do even a few months before. He did what he used to do back during his time at Saint Anthony's. He hid. He watched.

He crouched low on the roof of an old apartment building, scanning every bit of street, sidewalk, and alleyway he could see. And he sent out his friends, small, swift, numerous; they searched where he could not, and after hours of ignoring their own needs and hungers, they found what he was looking for, far above the streets of the city center, from the Viewpoint at Kerry Park.

The boy was a little older than Jove, tall and thin with a lot of very dark hair. He stood behind a short iron fence at the edge of the park overlooking the edge of Queen

Anne Hill, his eye pressed to the viewfinder of a camera with a long telephoto lens perched on a tripod. His jacket flapped around him in a light but steady breeze.

He trained the camera toward the city, but without peeking through the boy's eyes, Jove couldn't know what part of the city he was studying.

Jove dismissed his many flying friends and they gratefully went their own ways. There was still enough night left for them to feed.

He stood, stretching his legs, then his wings, and leapt into the air, himself grateful the night's long and idle search seemed to be over.

Jove's eyesight was sharp, not as sharp as his raven friends, but sharp enough to pick out the speck of a person on the distant cliff edge overlooking the city. He kept his eyes on the figure as he took flight, guiding himself to the Space Needle's observation deck by memory. He glided low over the smaller apartment complexes, then shot straight up, only feet from the dark glass surface of a deserted high-rise where the boy would be unable to spot him. When he was over the building, he made a speedy perpendicular course toward his favorite perch and saw movement behind the camera and tripod.

The boy had seen him.

Jove didn't land atop the observation deck. He sped past it, straight up into the night sky and climbed until the city became a phantom glow below the diffuse, low-hanging clouds.

Relying again on nothing but memory, and sometimes he wasn't even sure if it was his memory or the collective memory of his many little friends in the sky, Jove leveled out and drifted toward Kerry Park.

He'd decided that he would turn the table on his spy, and maybe, if the right opportunity presented itself, give the guy a scare he'd never forget.

But only if he was sure he could keep the monster inside under control.

Kaine waited for another hour before calling it a night. It was morning, actually, a few hours from sunrise, and he was bushed. These long nights were beginning to take a toll on him.

After the Puget Devil's very quick pass by the Space Needle, it had disappeared into the night sky. Another fruitless night, but Kaine didn't let that get him down. Some nights were a bust, but when he scored, it was usually big. His Puget Devil portfolio was busting with unused photos, some almost worthless, most passable if not outstanding. There were enough winners to keep that tabloid hack happy, probably more than he'd need. The American Star's interest in the Puget Devil would probably run out before his current supply of good photos.

So why am I still hunting it?

He paused in the act of loading his equipment into the trunk of Grandma Vicky's old Volvo. It was a disturbing question on more than one level, and one he thought he should try to answer while it was heavy on his mind.

Hunting. Was he hunting? Was this about the work now, little as it paid, though as he often reminded himself, the exposure and professional credits were worth more than the actual cash at this point in his career, or was it about getting *trophy* shots?

He had plans for a few of his photographs, other than building his portfolio. His favorite, the Puget Devil taking flight over the highest point of the Space Needle, silhouetted between the points of a crescent moon, would never make it to The American Star. He planned to blow that one up and give it to Uncle Chuckles as a gift, framed and ready to hang. He also thought he'd like to pick one out for himself, and maybe another for Grandma Vicky, though she wasn't nearly as invested in the legend as he and Uncle Chuckles were.

If it was nothing more than trophy hunting without a gun, he needed to stop, at least long enough to get the rest of his life into some kind of order. These long nights were killing his limited social life, and the part time dock job, which had paid more than his art and photography, had fallen to the wayside already. He didn't miss it much. It had been hard and boring work. His supervisor was a self-important prick, and his last shift the week before had been one of the most unpleasant days of his life, although the bit at the end when he told the old bastard to fuck off had been a bright spot.

Smiling at that memory, Kaine closed the trunk and climbed in, starting the aged Volvo's motor and turned the heat up full blast. It had been a chilly, overcast night, and even more than his bed, Kaine craved a little warmth.

So, there was a certain thrill to the hunt itself beyond any notoriety or monetary gain. Grandma Vicky was right when she said no one who hadn't seen the Puget Devil for themselves would believe his photos were real. There were the hardcore tabloid audience who believed anything they saw in print, but that wasn't the niche he wanted to serve.

So what else is there?

There was his irritation at Ty Scott, which had taken him somewhat by surprise. The guy wrote for The American Star, so Kaine had known from the start of their professional relationship that he wasn't going to be a shining example of truth.

The thing he kept snagging on was the reality of the Puget Devil. It was not The Weeping Jesus Taco Chip. It was real, whether Ty believed it or not. The reports Uncle Chuckles passed to him, and that he in turn had shared with Ty Scott, did not describe a bloodthirsty monster prowling the nighttime city, looking for virgins to eat. The Puget Devil seemed people shy, skittish, and the only reports of direct violence were against criminals, and though none of the reports said so implicitly, they suggested most of the attacks occurred during the commission of some crime.

There was no question about the convenience store incident. The Puget Devil had ignored the surviving employee and the police, even after they'd opened fire. The junkie who had tried to rob the place, killing one in the process, was no longer a problem. He was as dead as dead could be. He'd ended his life as a smear on the pavement.

Kaine finally understood, and laughed as he put the car in reverse. He backed out of his parking spot, the lone visitor to Kerry Park that early morning.

"I'm trying to catch him being a hero," he said, just to see if it sounded as silly aloud as it did in the privacy of his own thoughts.

Somehow it didn't. Aloud it sounded too plausible.

Not quite Kerry Park's lone visitor that early morning.

As Kaine drove away, turning onto the deserted street back toward the heart of the city, Jove leapt from the cover of a thick grove of trees and followed.

The drive southwest to the apartment was uneventful; the streets themselves seemed lonely and a little forlorn, as if missing all of the daytime hustle that fed them. He drove past the Space Needle on the way and wasn't able to resist an upward glance into the sky, but it was still empty.

Fifteen minutes later he was parked and walking to the front entrance of his apartment building when the strangest man he'd ever seen seemed to grow from the shadows.

"My good man," he said, sweeping a large and baggy knit cap from his head and spilling the unruliest tangle of dreadlocks Kaine had ever seen. "I'm looking for a place called Danforth Halls. I came to visit my old maiden Aunt Ida, but I don't want to wake her to find out of this is the place."

"This is it," Kaine said, though he kept back a few paces from the man, a short guy, plump and cheerful looking, but wearing an overlong and baggy duster that could conceal an arsenal of weapons. "Where are you from?"

Kaine waited for the guy to back off a bit, but he remained standing in front of the building's front steps.

"Me? I hail from far, far away, but I drove from Vegas. Nonstop except to piss and gas up."

"Hard drive, man." Kaine decided the man had no intentions of moving. He'd just have to squeeze past him.

The stranger laughed. "Son, I drive for a living. Driving is easy. The hard part is concentrating on the road when there's a sex starved succubus hiding in your pocket, tickling your taint."

This guy's a fucking goofball, Kaine decided, and moved to step around him. "Gotta go."

The stranger grabbed Kaine by the shoulder and turned him back around. The weirdo was strong.

"We're having a conversation son. Don't be rude."

Kaine leaned down to tell the guy to back the hell off (my, what big eyes you have) and suddenly his fear and anger were gone. He realized that he *had* been very rude. He should apologize.

"Sorry bro. Didn't mean to be a dick."

Offer him something, an urgent little voice inside his head insisted, and Kaine made a quick mental inventory of his pants pockets. He had a wallet with his license and about fifty bucks cash, a bit of loose change, the keys to Grandma Vicky's car …

Kaine fished the keys out and held them out. "Here, have my car."

The stranger laughed. "You hang onto those, Kaine. I've got a little job for you that requires wheels."

Jove watched his photographer speak to the strange little man, then turn around and walk back to his car. A few minutes later he was heading back the way he'd come, and Jove followed, puzzled by his sudden change of direction.

They followed the same route back into downtown, but instead of continuing to Queen Anne Hill and Kerry Park, he exited onto 6th avenue and turned right a few blocks further down Pike Street.

This part of the city didn't offer much cover, so Jove set down atop the taller of the Union Square Towers to watch his photographer's progress. He didn't drive much farther.

The photographer exited into the five-story car garage, and for the next few minutes was lost to sight.

Jove was contemplating flying down for a closer look when he spotted a speck of a human figure moving onto the roof. He closed his eyes, let his mind wander, and found a friend perched warily only yards away from the wandering photographer. Jove watched through his little friend's eyes.

Andy Crow watched and waited, hiding inside an open dumpster under the spot where the nosey little bastard with the camera would soon appear, pleased with how Charles's plan was going. They'd been watching The Puget Devil and his photographer for a few days now, and finally, finally his boy had caught the photographer's trail.

Andy was a little disappointed, actually. He'd have caught on long before now if someone was spying on him, and he wouldn't have wasted any time stalking the kid back to his home, no fucking way.

You fucked with Andrew Crow, you took a long, hard dive, and in a way, the photographer kid *was* fucking with him. The pictures he was producing could get a couple of wayfaring entrepreneurs like Mr. Greene and himself into a lot of trouble if they were seen by the wrong folks.

He owed Chuck one now, first for spotting the potential problem before it got out of hand, and now for a fairly simple plan that would remove the nosey photographer and his subject from the public eye with a minimum of fuss and noise.

That was the most important thing now; ending this absurd spectacle before someone decided to take it seriously. If the wider world of humans ever learned about the other worlds, or discovered one of the few remaining relics that led back and forth between them, his world would be overrun.

Fucking humans.

Weak they may be, but there were so damned many of them. They reproduced themselves like roaches and destroyed everything they touched.

And they call us *monsters*, Andy marveled.

Humans were the real monsters, stupid, smug little monkeys with just enough knowledge to be dangerous. Like the proverbial dog that finally catches the car, you had to pity anyone else who shared the road with them if they ever figured out how to drive the damn thing.

The kid photographer would shortly be bottled up with that old biddy he lived with, and *his* kid …

Andy still wasn't certain what to do about Little Andy Junior, or whatever the kid's name turned out to be.

Shocking as it was, the other races were supposed to be biologically incompatible with the monkeys, his kid was half-human. Andy's son or not, he'd already displayed the dual human frailties of inattention and gullibility that night.

If the boy could be taught though, reconditioned out of his human weaknesses, sharpened up a bit, he would make a fine addition to team Crow. If he, Andy, were able to move about as one of *them* during the daytime, well just imagine the possibilities.

Watching Kaine Moran approach the edge of the high roof, tensing for the right moment to leave his hiding place and join the events about to unfold five floors above the bustling city, Andy decided that when they made it to California to start that cult thingy Chuck was so excited about, well, Chuck could play God and Andy would relegate himself to the part of … what? Servant to the divine? God's favorite angel?

Something like that.

People are dumb. They'll swallow just about any old turd you hand them if you smile and tell them it's candy.

Charles was on the move, not precisely following Kaine, he didn't want to be so close as to present an obvious target to Andy's do-gooder of a kid, but moving in that general direction. He didn't need to hurry. A nice leisurely pace should bring him to the right place at roughly the right moment, if all went according to plan. It was a rough plan, but rough was just how Charles preferred it.

He followed Kaine's route to the all-night parking

garage, could see it just a block ahead in fact, and was prepared to keep circling it until his plan succeeded or failed.

Personally, he was betting on success. If his instincts about Andy's kid were right, and his instincts usually were, the little winged upstart would take the bait without a thought. After that, it was all up to Andy, and Andy never failed.

Never. You could count on him.

The streets were mostly empty. Good.

Charles turned his van right, starting his first circuit around the building Kaine should be in, or on, at that very moment.

Kaine, what a cool name, Charles thought.

He'd been scooting around under the Charles Greene moniker for a while now. Maybe it was time for a change. Kaine Moran had a nice ring to it - dark and rock-n-roll-ish, with a jolly Irish flourish.

The van's back door, rolled all the way up so the cargo area was open to the night, rattled in its track. The other door, their *special* door, stood open as well. Four sturdy ratchet straps held its frame upright, anchored to eye-hooks on the ceiling and floor.

Anyone who looked inside the van as it passed would be looking straight through that open door and into another world.

Andy waited for Kaine Moran's signal. If all went according to plan, and he had no reason to believe it wouldn't, he'd have a few seconds to wait once the signal was sent. He had no reason to doubt Chuck's plan. When Charles Greene locked eyes with someone, he was very persuasive.

He probably wouldn't even need the signal, he had a straight line of sight to the spot and his eyesight was exquisite, but it never hurt to be safe.

The signal came, a voice from high above, and Andy clicked his beak in anticipation.

"Goodbye, cruel world!"

Andy was surprised into a short laugh. Leave it to Chuck. Everything was a joke to old Charles Greene.

Kaine came into view then, directly above him, exactly where Chuck said he would be. He stood for a moment, seeming to totter on the edge, as if some part of his real self recognized what he was about to do and fought to stop it, then Kaine put one foot out and stepped forward into thin air.

"Goodbye, cruel world!"

Kaine heard his own voice, understood the words, and would have laughed if he could have. Kind of a funny thing to say, he thought.

He wondered briefly why he had said it, and remembered the short guy with the funny eyes.

He had been very pleasant, that guy. Cool hair too. Very long and wiggly.

Now walk.

The suggestion, a command really, was too strong to resist, but when he focused forward again, down at his feet and the empty air in front of him, he tried to resist it anyway.

He thought he might have hesitated for just a short moment, but that could have been wishful thinking, because the next thing Kaine knew, he was tipping over the edge of a tall building, not the tallest in the city, but tall enough, and falling toward the street below.

Thanks, and have a lovely night, the controlling voice in his brain said, and then Kaine was all himself again.

He screamed as the ground rushed up at him.

Jove watched in confusion as his photographer crossed the roof to the very edge and made his melodramatic pronouncement, then in horror when he stepped over the edge and fell toward the ground five stories below.

Jove didn't hesitate. He acted quickly, decisively, without a thought, and though he was half a block away and several stories higher than the photographer, Jove had hold of him before the fall was half over.

It was still a close thing, despite Jove's speed. There was a brief tug of war with gravity over the falling body, but Jove won, clutching the screaming photographer in his arms as he leveled out and skimmed the blacktop.

Then a bang behind them alerted him, and he turned hiis head in time to see something huge and blacker than the night around them burst from the open lid of a dumpster.

Huge, black, and winged.

A second later it was on top of them, and Jove found

himself crushed in the new monster's powerful arms, the prey now instead of the predator.

Andy resisted the urge to crow as he wrapped his long arms around his prey, crushing them to his chest. A few beats of his wings took them higher into the air, and after a brief search, he spotted Chuck's van cruising along not a half-block away.

He pumped his wings again and shot toward the open bay door like a black missile. A few seconds later he was inside the van, and a second after that he was through the other door, the special door, carrying his captives into another world.

Charles heard the thump and felt the van rock as several hundred pounds of giant bird and scrawny, long-haired photographer landed. Damn near flawless, he marveled, peeking into the rear-view mirror as the cargo door rattled in its tracks and slammed shut. He'd been treated to the very brief image of Andy dexterously tugging the door down with the long talons of one foot, while he balanced on the other, both his captives held tight in his long arms.

He even thought Andy gave him a sly wink just before vanishing through the door to their home. Then that door also slammed, and Charles pulled up to the curb. This was only a precaution, the odds of the junior birdman and the human overpowering Andy and coming back through the door were beyond slim, but you didn't get as far in life as Charles did by not eliminating the unnecessary risks.

He squeezed through the opening into the cargo area, cursing as he fell through onto the hard, wooden floor.

"Fuck a duck," he said, rising and dusting himself off. He swept his cap off and seemed to concentrate for a moment as the tangle of dreadlocks rippled and moved. At last one untangled itself from the mass and stretched itself out, wrapped around the shaft of a small brass key. Charles fit the key into the brass plate beneath the lock, gave it a twist, then withdrew it.

Their business in Seattle was almost finished now. He climbed back into the cab, not bothering to replace his cap. Sometimes it was nice to just let it all hang out. The cap was necessary. Some people did notice that his hair, if you looked close enough, didn't actually look like hair, so he had to keep it covered around the natives.

It was nighttime now, they weren't in company, and he wouldn't be driving far anyway.

Before pulling back onto the road, he rolled his window down. A little wind through his *hair* would feel good about now.

He decided to pitch his California idea to Andy again, and take some time and to visit the Mojave before dropping down into LA if they went. The Mojave had such wonderful cactuses.

CHAPTER 9

The first thing Kaine noticed about his new surroundings was the painting he'd given Vicky, the panoramic Seattle cityscape, hanging from a wall that wasn't really a wall. The wall was stone, uneven and shot through with fissures. The second thing he noticed was the wall itself, then the sparse furnishings, a desk complete with laptop, a leather recliner, and then the sofa he was slumped on.

The third thing he noticed was the boy, sleeping on the other end of the sofa, a small, scrawny kid, maybe thirteen or fourteen. He was slumped over the sofa's overstuffed arm, a blanket draped over his pathetically malnourished stick-figure of a body. It was one of those touristy Native American things, colorful and rustic and crammed with dancing stick-figure Indians. The kind of thing you'd find in a Southwest tourist trap, made by some old woman on the reservation and selling for three or four hundred dollars.

Kaine groaned and sat up, immediately regretting the movement. He closed his eyes and braced himself against a monster headache that threatened to pop his head like an overstrained water balloon. He tried to remember how he'd ended up in this position, hungover and feeling he'd been wrung out. There was no memory that might explain his current condition.

Maybe I got so fucked up I blacked out.

But even as the thought occurred to him, he dismissed it. He didn't drink that often, and never that much. Well, almost never. He had certainly never blacked out.

And that boy on the other end of the couch, Kaine had a feeling he might be naked under that blanket.

Too creepy.

When his head felt a little less likely to explode from any sudden movement, he opened his eyes again and scanned the room around him.

It was huge, wide open, dimly lit by maybe a thousand strands of Christmas lights, tiny white bulbs that hung like icicles from the ceiling. Spaced evenly between the lights were hundreds of small limestone daggers, hanging point down from the ceiling. Here and there larger ones reached toward the floor, which was flat, though not perfectly so.

This isn't a room, it's a cavern.

Then the chair on the other side of the desk moved, spun around, and the short little man he'd met outside his apartment (it was beginning to come back now, meeting this weird man and then falling from the top of a building, those were his last memories) was facing him, grinning so widely his face looked like it was cramping.

"Boy, you really should see the look on your face right now."

"Charles Greene." Charles held out a hand, as if this were nothing more unusual than a job interview, and put on a look of deep hurt when Kaine didn't move forward to take it. Then he shrugged and grinned again, as if moving on. "I'm a great fan of your work … a collector, you could say."

Charles slid out the top desk drawer and removed a stack of magazines, every issue of The American Star featuring Kaine's pictures of The Puget Devil. Next, he pulled out a stack of photo albums, the ones Kaine kept all of his originals and negatives in.

"Even your unpublished work has a certain gritty realism to it." Charles winked. "Of course, you and I both know that's because they *are* real."

He threw his pudgy, short fingered hands high in the air and turned his face toward the cavern's ceiling like an evangelist getting ready for a good god shout.

"Halleluiah, monsters are real," then he looked down at Kaine again, "and you've got photographic evidence."

He stood, gripping the edge of the desk, and leaned forward over his collection of Kaine's photos.

"And frankly son, it's beginning to piss us off."

Kaine faced the strange man for a silent, stunned moment, then finally found his voice. "Sir, I don't know what the hell you're talking about."

"Oh, but I think you do, my boy." Charles relaxed back into his seat again and spun it round a few times. "I do suppose we have you to thank for alerting us to the existence of our mutual friend sitting next to you, and for helping us locate him, but our gratitude only stretches so far."

Kaine stood slowly, testing his legs and Charles's reactions. His legs worked, they supported him a little reluctantly, but he was able to stay upright, and Charles made no objection to him moving. The strange man watched Kaine with interest as he closed half the distance between them.

"Who is that?" Kaine hooked a thumb back over his shoulder toward the sleeping boy. "And what does he have to do with me?"

"At the moment I'm calling him Andy Junior, until he's able to tell me his proper name. I know a lot about him, but he never thinks of himself in the first person, so I couldn't get his name. You know him as The Puget Devil."

"Bullshit," Kaine blurted before he was able to control himself. He looked back, and the boy still slept soundly. His eyes moved rapidly behind their lids, as if he were having very active dreams.

"I assure you it is not bullshit. He is in fact the number one son of a good friend of mine."

"Andy Senior," Kaine guessed.

Charles laughed. "Yes indeed. Andy was all for just disposing of you in the usual fashion, like your writer friend, and I gotta admit, it's not a bad way to go. Lisa's sex drive can be a bit demanding though, and when her boy toys start having trouble keeping up with her demands she gets a little psychotic."

Kaine puzzled over that for a moment, he didn't have

any writer friends, then remembered Ty from The American Star.

"You've got Ty Scott down here?" Unable to help himself, Kaine snuck another quick look at the boy. His eyes were half open now, sweeping the strange room sleepily.

"We know him as Doug," Charles corrected. "Yep, Lisa's been having fun with him for a few days, but I think the good times are just about over for him. He's all skin and bones now and all he does now is groan and scream."

Kaine had no idea what the strange little man was talking about, but it didn't sound good.

"I'm all for sending you and grandma home. I'd have to diddle your brains a bit though."

"*You've got my grandma?*" Kaine closed the distance between them in a few quick strides and reached across the desk. He got a fistful of the little man's over-long duster and yanked him from his seat. "Where is she?"

Charles only continued to grin his abnormal ear-to-ear grin, unperturbed by Kaine's manhandling. Kaine was about to give him a shake when he felt something cold press against his forehead. He'd never had a gun pointed at him, let alone had one pressed to his skin, but Kaine didn't need to see the cold ring of metal pressed to his forehead to know what it was.

"You're not helping your case you know," Charles scolded. But he didn't look at all upset. He looked like he was having fun.

Kaine let him go and slowly raised his hands.

The cold ring of metal disappeared, and Kaine saw a small pistol pointing at his face, held steady, impossibly, by one of Charles's long dreadlocks.

Another snaked out from beneath his leaning cap, gripping an unsheathed dagger by its handle.

"Go have a seat," Charles said. He smiled wider, a friendly, encouraging smile. "Come on amigo, you need to relax."

The small pistol nudged Kaine's nose, and he backed toward the couch.

The dreadlock holding the knife slithered back under his baggy cap. The gun did not vanish, but the living dreadlock pointed it at the ceiling instead of him, which was an improvement.

"Ah, our young friend is awake at last," Charles nearly shouted. He clapped enthusiastically. The million little lights above and around them blinked out, then came on again.

They have The Clapper, Kaine thought, and stifled the urge to giggle.

"Mister Crow will be tickled."

Kaine turned to see the boy, wrapped in his colorful blanket, standing at the other end of the couch. He ignored Kaine, glared at Charles.

"Where's Crow? Where's the birdman?"

Jove listened to the conversation for a minute before allowing himself to open his eyes and take in the strange surroundings. It was his photographer and the weird little man he'd met with earlier that night. A man who called himself Charles Greene.

Jove awakened mid-conversation and hadn't gotten

much from it, but he knew that name from somewhere. It rang a bell with him, faint but insistent.

Kaine, the photographer's name was Kaine, had done something to piss Greene and his friend Andy off … something about pictures and monsters.

Me, of course, Jove thought. *But why?*

Jove opened his eyes just enough to scan his surroundings, and caught Kaine looking at him, then Kaine turned his attention back to Greene.

Greene … where did he know that name?

Then Kaine shouted, startling Jove into full wakefulness. Kaine rushed to the desk where Greene sat and reached over it, pulling the little man from his seat.

Jove tensed for the coming fight, but didn't move. He was very aware of his weak human body. How long had he been out anyway? Long enough for the sun to come up, he guessed.

But the fight didn't happen. Kaine let Greene go and put his hands in the air, backing slowly away, and Jove saw the strange tentacles that looked like hair rising in thick strands around Greene's loose cap. They twisted and angled through the air like snakes, one holding a gun on Kaine, another waving a knife.

He smiled his daffy smile at Kaine, then caught Jove's eye. His smile widened.

"Ah, our young friend is awake at last," he said, speaking louder than before, including Jove in the conversation. He clapped, and the dreadlock holding the gun began to twirl it like a Wild West gunfighter. The lights above and around them turned off, then on again with each echoing crack of his palms. "Mister Crow will be tickled."

Crow?

And Jove understood how he knew Greene's name now, understood why it had pinged off his memory so sharply

Crow and Greene. He had their business card in his small horde of possessions at his room.

He stood, wrapping the small blanket tightly around his body. He still wore his baggy grey shorts, but his back was bare beneath the blanket, and he didn't like people looking at his wings. It was embarrassing.

If Greene smiled any wider the top of his head would tip right off and land behind him.

"Where's Crow?" Jove said. "Where's the birdman?"

"He'll be with us soon, young man," Greene said, dropping into a bow. "He's quite excited to meet you, but he needed a bit of alone time."

Andy Crow stalked around the lower levels of the cave complex he called home. Not the *lowest* level, where he kept the generator, but close enough that he could hear its hum and feel its vibration through the cavern floor. This was the level where he kept prisoners, including the bag of bones and spunk that Lisa was currently draining, and the photographer kid's grandma. They'd been kinder to her than most they'd brought down here. Andy didn't think her heart would take another scare like the one he'd thrown at her in her apartment, so Chuck had worked his magic and the lady was currently snoozing soundly at the bottom of the most comfortable pit. She had a cot to stretch out on and everything.

Not too far away he could hear Lisa screwing the last little bit of life out of the writer. He'd finally quit screaming. Now he just grunted a lot.

She was going to be furious when she found out he was tossing the kid back.

He sighed and clicked his beak in irritation.

Oh well, he'd have to make it up to her. He'd make sure she got some good play time in when they set up in California.

It was never a good idea to let Lisa get too hungry. The succubus was loyal enough, but a girl had to eat.

"I'm hungry for love," Andy hummed. "Like a ..."

Lisa's moans became shrieks of pleasure, and somehow the writer found the strength to scream again. It was long, piercing, echoing around the stone chamber until it became an a cappella chorus of pleasure and pain. Her shrieks continued while his petered off into low choked moans.

There are worse ways to go, Andy reminded himself.

He paced around the chamber, trying to put a little more distance between himself and the fatal case of coitus maximus going on in the writer's pit, as if it would help.

He turned to the wall of security monitors positioned against the entrance wall, each placed in its own cubical on the high shelf, and found the one showing a wide angle of the mostly empty lobby. He wished they'd wired it for sound, he could see the photographer speaking rather animatedly with Chuck but would like to have heard their conversation.

The boy, his boy, lay sleeping against the arm of the sofa.

Andy paced between the pits, glancing down into

them one by one. All empty but two now, it had been a long time since the place was this empty, but once they settled the situation at hand they'd start filling them up again.

He glanced back up at the monitor and stopped pacing.

The boy was awake now, rising from the couch.

Time to get it over with.

Andy leapt, pumping his wings once and sailing across the low chamber to the pit with the photographer's grandmother.

Be gentle, he reminded himself, and scooped her from her cot before leaping back out of the pit.

He moved quickly now, not quite running. He left the prison room behind and moved through the dimly lit corridor that spiraled back toward the surface world. Not this woman's world, but his. He raced toward the lobby, the top-most chamber of the complex, feeling an unfamiliar flutter of dread in his stomach.

He was nervous. This daddy shit was very new to him.

CHAPTER 10

"Yes, the big guy has arrived!" Charles Greene shouted with pleasure and motioned toward a dark patch in the distant wall of stone, a low passage into the corridor beyond.

Kaine gasped and staggered back a step. His legs hit the edge of the couch and he dropped onto it. He looked a bit swoony to Charles, but he couldn't blame the kid. Most people got a bit faint the first time they saw Andy.

Jove handled himself a little better, but Charles had expected he would. He was used to monsters by now, having been one himself for a few years. The boy tensed when Andy entered the chamber but didn't lose control of his limbs.

Andy Crow ducked through the low passage into the huge main chamber, then straightened to his impressive eight feet. The woman in his arms slept serenely, not even stirring when he unfurled his wings and leapt into the air. For a moment he was nothing but a black blur passing beneath the lit dome of the high ceiling, then he touched down gently a few feet in front of Kaine.

Kaine found his breath and used it spectacularly.

"Vicky!" A second later he found his legs too, and leapt up to charge Andy. It was the first time in many years Charles had seen a mere human move in any direction but away from Andy, under their own power at least. "You killed her!"

Kaine drew back his fist to punch, a ballsy move Chuck had to admit, but a silly one. His fist would have reached no higher than Andy's stomach if it had landed.

It didn't land, with a brief twitch of his wing, Andy swept Kaine aside, then lay the sleeping woman on the couch. He turned to Kaine, sprawled on the floor, eyes still on his grandma.

"She's not dead, you dolt. Don't do that again."

Andy turned to Charles, still sitting behind the desk, straining to hold back laughter, and winked. Then he turned to Jove and bent low to look him in the face.

"Funny, he doesn't look a thing like me."

———

Jove stared back into the face of Andrew Crow and felt no anger or fear. Only curiosity.

He had expected anger; anger over the death of his mother, anger over his abandonment at Saint Anthony's. Anger for being left on his own.

He'd expected fear, and he knew that he should be afraid, but he just couldn't be.

All of the unanswered questions he'd had since his sometimes frightening, sometimes exhilarating transformations started could be answered by this … not a man, but not the demon he'd expected either.

Monster, then. Like Jove himself.

"Funny," Andy Crow said, "he doesn't look a thing like me."

He unfurled his wings again, tensed them as if stretching, then folded them flat to his back. With his wings tucked out of sight he looked much more like a man.

The birdman cocked his head to the side and clicked his beak, as if he'd seen something yummy, a big fat worm maybe, slithering on the floor and was considering snapping it up before it crawled away.

A little more like a man, Jove reconsidered.

"Give him another hour or so. Once the sun sets the resemblance will become very pronounced," Charles reassured him.

Andy nodded. "I know."

"Look at his back," Charles advised. "You will be amazed, I promise."

Jove braced himself for the rough hands that would seize him and spin him around, tearing the blanket from his back, but his father did not move.

"May I?" Andy asked, and Jove found himself momentarily speechless at the unexpected politeness.

He nodded and slipped the blanket off his shoulders.

Andy took him by the shoulder, gently, and turned him around. For a moment the chamber was silent, then Andy sucked a whistle in through his beak.

"That is something else," he said at last, and turned Jove around to face him again. "You know who I am?"

"Yeah, I know," Jove said.

"Do you know *what* I am?"

"I don't even know what *I* am," Jove said, and a small measure of the anger he'd expected finally rose.

Andy nodded.

"I imagine you're a bit pissed off right now, aren't you? Being on your own all this time. The orphanage ...," Andy chuckled, "thinking you were turning into some kind of old testament demon."

Jove's lip curled up, revealing teeth yellowed from neglect.

Andy patted his shoulder. "I'm not laughing at you son, just the situation. My good friend Chuck had a peek inside your thinker after he put you to sleep and brought me up to speed on your interesting life."

"He did what?"

"It's a talent of his," Andy said. "He's a member of a rare breed, a south island cult of ... monks I guess."

"Close enough," Charles said. For once his ever-present smile was gone. His wide, flabby mouth hung in a frown and he hunched forward in his chair, sulking.

"Reclusive, this bunch, race almost extinct, spend years at a time in trance with each other seeking the mysteries of the multiverse, and Mr. Greene here was something of a disappointment to them." Andy turned to regard Charles. "Their loss, my friend."

Charles perked up a bit at his friend's words, but his reciprocating smile was a little less than full wattage.

Andy stood and began to pace the empty floor.

"They considered him too undisciplined. His thoughts were too random for them. Too ... base."

"I'm bug-fuck crazy," Charles confided, tipping Kaine, who watched the exchange in confused silence, a huge wink.

"They disagreed with his unique world view that God spends his time wrapped in the warm folds of a cosmic vagina."

Kaine laughed against his will and slapped a hand over his mouth.

Jove regarded the little man with growing distaste.

"He's a pervert," Andy clarified. "Which in his old sect was a crime punishable by death."

"This fella," Charles said, motioning to Andy, "who incidentally is not as rare in this world as you may think, and far from the scariest hombre wandering these strange and exotic lands, rescued me from a fate worse than simple death."

"They were particularly displeased with him," Andy agreed. "They didn't just want him dead. They wanted him erased, memory by memory."

"Go on," Charles said, his enthusiasm for the conversation growing. He was beginning to look pleased with the memories now rather than depressed by them. "Young master Jove is a friend, and Kaine here won't remember a word we say once this is over."

Jove shot a quick look at Kaine, who was now sitting by the edge of the couch beside his sleeping grandmother.

Andy considered his friend for a moment, then shrugged his massive, feathered shoulders.

"When Chuck here gets in your head he doesn't just see and experience your memories, he can rearrange them, change them, influence your thoughts and behavior. It's a handy talent, but those big, earnest eyes of his are also his weakness, just like the rest of his race. Stick an undisciplined south island monk in front of a mirror long enough and he can't help but look."

"It's unsettling," Charles said, "seeing that clearly into your own head. You see things you don't care for much. Before long you begin eating your own memories, and once you start, it's damn hard to stop."

Charles stood and leaned over his desk, once again grinning his too-wide grin. "But enough about me, Andy. I think the boy would rather hear about you."

Andy stopped his pacing to consider Jove, who nodded once and waited in silence.

"Hey, you … kid!" Charles motioned toward Kaine, then waved him over. "Come on kid … Andy's the biter, not me."

"Go on," Andy encouraged. "We've already decided not to kill you. He just wants to discuss your work."

Charles nodded seriously. "You're pretty good, but I think you're wasting your talent."

Kaine shot a questioning look at Jove, who could only shrug in return, then rose on unsteady legs and walked to Charles.

"Seattle at night is a bit passé. There's a whole world out there waiting to be captured. Take the Mojave Desert's flowering cactuses …"

Andy took Jove by the shoulder and led him away from the lightly snoring woman on the couch. Charles's chattering on the virtues of flowering cactuses faded into the background.

"So, where should I start?"

"From the middle," Jove said. He had a feeling it would be a long story.

Andy nodded as if he approved. "Just the essentials for now." He ducked back into the low passage, then straightened up on the other side. It was narrow, but tall enough to admit Andy's tall frame with room to spare.

Jove followed warily.

"Where are we going?"

"Looking for a spot of sky," Andy said. "I just want to see where the sun's at."

Jove wondered that too. His stunted wings were twitching under the blanket in a way he recognized well enough.

"Strictly speaking you and I come from the same world. We're just native to different planes of probability on the same chunk of rock."

Jove replayed his father's words in his head as they walked and found they made no more sense. "Probability of what?"

"Exactly," Andy said.

The tunnel split ahead, one path turning down toward deeper darkness, the other awash in the first natural light Jove had seen for days, since the trip into Seattle's streets where he found the magazine with his picture on the cover.

"I don't get it," Jove said.

"That's okay, neither do I. Not completely anyway. But you don't need to understand it now, just accept it. Just keep your brain trained of the big picture view of reality. The little shit takes care of itself without our corroboration."

If there was a response to that, Jove didn't know what it was. He kept silent and followed Andy toward the light.

"Third rock from the star Sol. That's the starting point.

We both come from there, only the one you're familiar with gave up magic a long time ago. The people there traded magic for dogma, and when dogma failed to provide real solutions for real problems, the monkeys who live there strained their brains and discovered technological progress." Andy stopped to consider the degree of light pouring in from the unseen opening still far in the distance. "It's really a pretty good trick considering where they started. I gotta respect that about them if nothing else."

The light seemed to come from above, shining down some out of sight shaft. Jove thought he heard a bird twitter in the distance, somewhere above them in the daylight.

"The third rock I'm most familiar with doesn't have much in the way of humans, for which every other race is grateful, and we don't have technology, but we do have magic still, and a few who can still use it."

Andy turned to look at Jove for the first time since leading him out of the big chamber.

"And no," he said, answering Jove's unspoken question, "I'm not one of them. Neither, I suspect, are you. But that's okay. I bet you'll get by okay without it."

Andy bent and scooped a stone from the floor, spinning it between the tips of his taloned fingers.

"Same rock, different worlds."

"Like Heaven and Hell?"

"Not even close," Andy said, chuckling. "Different histories. Different paths."

"How do you get from mine to yours?"

"Relics," Andy said with a dismissive wave of his hand. The stone sailed into the darkness behind them and rolled out of sight. "Things left behind … traps maybe, no idea who made them or how, but I got my hands on one of them a long time ago and followed it into your world. Turned my new toy into a profitable business.

"We're head hunters. We find a specific kind of people and recruit them for service to third parties. Sometimes we track down fugitives who think they can hide out on your side."

Andy continued toward the light, and Jove followed.

"It's a tricky proposition, and I hate to come down hard on you but you're making it trickier flying around all over the place and getting photographed."

They were there now, not the end of the cavern, but directly underneath the shaft that led to the surface world. Sunlight fell on Andy's oil black body and seemed to slide off him like water. Jove blinked and shaded his eyes.

Andy stood for a moment, facing up into the light.

"If the monkeys found out about this world … if they found one of the relics that led here, it would be bedlam."

Andy grabbed Jove under his armpits and lifted him until they were face to face. "The folks I answer to here would have our heads on poles."

"Let me go!" Jove beat his fists against Andy's chest. It was like punching a feathery boulder. He kicked out, but his feet swished uselessly through the air.

"Relax, I'm not going to eat you." And he leapt straight up, keeping his wings tucked tightly to his back. A second later, or so it felt to Jove, they were standing in the grass of a forest clearing at the granite foot of a mountain.

Jove turned where he stood to take in his surroundings, and gasped.

"That's Mount Rainer."

"Almost," Andy said, and a moment later something huge, titanic, dropped from the clouds and landed on the peak. "You won't see any of those on Mount Rainer."

"What is it?" He'd read that the largest animal on Earth was the blue whale, and the thing now crawling around the high peak of Not Mount Rainer appeared to be several times larger. Jove shrank back and bumped into Andy, then stepped away from him quickly.

"We can talk about that some other time. The important thing is that you realize you're not in Kansas anymore."

"What?"

"Never mind."

More silence as Jove ate the landscape up with his eyes.

I am standing on a different world, he thought.

The sun sat low and bloated on what he could only assume was the western horizon. The moon was already on the rise to the east.

His wings twitched, and he wondered what sights he'd see in these new skies.

He also wondered if the thing slinking off to the far side of the mountain's high peak was a carnivore.

"Jove?"

Jove turned and found Andy crouched on one knee and leaning low, almost on the same level as him.

"What?"

"I'm sorry, but you're not going back."

Jove nodded. He'd already known that.

"You can hang around with us if you'd like, join Team Crow." He laughed briefly. The sounds startled strange insects from the tall grass around them. "Or you can go off on your own if you can't stomach our company."

Jove folded his arms across the blanket covering his chest. He had not expected a choice of any kind. He wondered what the conditions might be, but he didn't have to wonder for long.

"If you decide to go off on your own, you get to take the old lady with you." Andy stared unblinking into Jove's eyes. "She won't last long in this world, no matter how closely you watch her, how much you look after her. She will die. You probably will too."

"What about Kaine?"

"We give Kaine to Lisa. She's just about finished with her current playmate … the one who wrote all that awful shit about you. Kaine's younger, got more juice, so he'll last a while longer. She'll take him again and again until there's nothing left. There are worse deaths I suppose." He shrugged and straightened up. "But that's rarely a comfort to the poor sap having his soul sucked out through his penis."

Jove tried not to think about it too deeply.

"If you agree to stay with us then Charles will give them some nice shiny new memories of the last few days and send them on home. They won't remember us, and you will have saved them from an unpleasant fate. But Charles has made me aware of your tendency for heroics, so I will be as plain as I can … we are not the good guys, and we never will be."

The sun dipped lower, then winked out as a blanket of low gray clouds covered it.

Night had arrived, or something close enough to night to suit Jove's strange biology.

A shiver ran up Jove's spine, and he groaned with discomfort as his body shifted smoothly and quickly from boy to monster. It wasn't the agony he'd experience the first few times, but the change was never what he'd call entirely comfortable.

"Oh," Andy said, taking a step back as he rose to his full height. "That was *very* slick!"

Jove stared up into his father's face, the rising moon lighting the oil black eyes. He saw his own face, identical in every way, reflected back at him in them. He let his blanket drop to the ground and stretched his wings out. They were fully formed and eager to face the night. He regarded his father, the villain Andrew Crow, and noted the baggy Bermuda shorts.

I need to get some of those ... mine are getting kind of gross.

"I'll stay with you," Jove said, as he already knew he'd have to.

But he wasn't going to take up a sidekick roll in the family business. He'd already decided that.

By the time that night was over, with any luck, his father and Charles might wish they'd left him alone.

CHAPTER 11

Kaine was out again; sleeping with his eyes open, his shallow breathing wanting to become a snore. Docile and boring.

He'd livened up a bit after Andy and Jove left. Livened up quite a bit actually. Kid came at him with a respectable roundhouse that would have knocked him out of his seat if it had landed. And he must have seemed like such an easy target, reclined with his feet up and his hands behind his head. People always seemed to forget about his extra appendages if he didn't whip them out every so often. It was like humans had a blind spot in their memories for things they couldn't quite cope with.

He'd caught the kid's fist and arm mid-swing, his tentacles wrapping tightly around them and yanking him forward. He pulled the boy toward him until they were face to face, and that was it. All the fight left the boy and he went all stiffish when Charles let him go.

Charles remained in his chair, leaning back, his legs crossed and his old boots resting on the desk. He held

Kaine's blank stare and slowly scrubbed away the memories Andy didn't want him carrying back to Seattle. His job was mostly finished. What he was adding now was just for him. He was currently implanting false but fond feelings toward the Mojave and its varied types of cactuses.

When he was finished, Kaine would be as wild about cactuses as he was, and his passé cityscapes would be a thing of the past.

This boy was going to be the Ansel Adams of cacti!

He finished and let his eyes drift toward the scuffed toes of his old boots. They needed a polish, and the soles were starting to wear thin again.

"You know how old these boots are?" He didn't look at Kaine when he spoke. He'd done quite enough rooting around in the poor kid's melon. You screwed with a guy's head too much and you were apt to leave holes in his identity, and once a person started fixating on the odd gaps in their mind they ended up losing what was left of it.

No need to be needlessly cruel to the boy. After all, it really was nothing personal.

Kaine did not reply, did not even respond to the sound of Charles's voice.

"Give you a hint," Charles said, smiling widely as he reclined further back and turned his face to the cavern ceiling. "In 1995 some folks dug up Jesse James's grave to see if it was really him down there. Most of him was gone, even the coffin they planted him in was mostly dirt by then, but the canvas sneakers on his bony feet were still in pretty good shape. They kept a lid on that part. Didn't want the media to find out someone beat them to the old boy."

Charles laughed at the memory.

Kaine seemed unimpressed.

Charles tapped the toes of the old boots together.

Quality craftsmanship," he said. "They'll be kicking up dust long after I *am* dust."

Soft, echoing footsteps alerted him to Andy's return.

He chanced a glance at Kaine, careful not to catch the kid's eyes.

Kaine continued to stare blankly through him.

"Go stand over there, kid." Charles pointed at the couch where Kaine's grandmother slept on, oblivious to all. "You're starting to bother me."

Kaine shuffled obediently toward the couch and stood, staring at the door standing a few feet away. It was set in a sturdy frame and braced from behind by a rough lumber scaffold.

Charles felt only a moment of unease as Kaine faced the door, then remembered the knob was safely in his top desk drawer. The relic, twin to the one in the back of their van, was their key back into that profitable other world. It would be bad if the kid regained his senses and escaped, but Charles had made sure that couldn't happen.

"All finished in here?" Andy emerged from the darkness of the corridor, and for a moment Charles thought he was alone.

The kid had flown the coop. That was a shocker, given what Charles knew about the altruistic little guy. Then a patch of darkness seemed to peel away from Andy's shadowy form, a smaller version of Big Andy, and walked at his side.

So, it was finished, the deal made, father and son reunited.

It was almost enough to bring tears to his eyes.

Once the monkeys, as Andy liked to call them, were back safely on the other side Charles thought he'd have a little celebration. A toke and a poke. He had developed a bit of a taste for higher end call girls over the years, and with his special powers of persuasion every ride was a free one.

"Almost," Charles said. "His brain is currently on hold. I'll finish up once they're back home sweet home."

Andrew and Jove Crow crossed the large empty space at a relaxed pace.

They were going to make one hell of a team.

"So, my fine boy, did the birdman answer all of your questions?"

All but one, Jove thought, but only because he hadn't asked it. It was an important one, but asking it would give him away. He thought he knew the answer, hoped he did anyway. Very soon he'd know one way or the other.

"He answered enough of them," Jove said.

They stopped in front of the desk, Andy resting a hand on Jove's shoulder.

"Thanks, old friend," his father said, and Jove could easily hear the emotion in that high and reedy voice. "Thank you for helping me find my son."

"Think nothing of it," Charles replied, dropping his feet to the floor and standing beside the desk. "It was a pleasure."

Charles leaned forward across the desk and held out a hand. A little reluctantly, Jove extended his in return. Charles shook it with enthusiasm.

"Welcome to the team, Jove. Welcome to the family."

And Jove was stunned to see tears welling up in the strange little man's eyes. Eyes that never did quite meet his own.

These two are like brothers, Jove thought. It seemed strange to him, but maybe it shouldn't. Maybe monsters need family too.

It was what he'd always wanted.

"Do I get to call you Uncle Chuck?"

Charles froze with his hand still outstretched, then burst into laughter. Weird laughter, slightly insane laughter, but genuine and contagious. Beside him, his father laughed too.

The honest joy in their laughter made Jove feel a little guilty for what he was about to do, but it was good to know these two were capable of forming attachments and feeling emotion.

"Sure kid," Charles said, wiping tears of laughter from under his wide and talented eyes. "Whatever blows your skirt up."

"Blows my skirt up?"

"Don't worry, son," his father said, releasing his shoulder and stepping around to the other side of the desk. He slid, a little uncomfortably it seemed, into Charles's vacated seat and slid open the top center drawer. "You'll get used to him."

Charles backed off a few paces, and when Andy addressed him, did not meet his friend's gaze. His eyes skittered across Andy's face, over the desktop, then settled on the object in his father's hand.

A doorknob, old and tarnished, inscribed with well-worn lines and symbols. It seemed to glow slightly as it changed hands.

"Time to send our guests home," Andy said. "Right back to their front door, then get us back on the road."

"And after that?" Charles looked anxious, hopeful.

"I'm thinking Los Angeles."

Charles's grin stretched too wide to seem possible. It was a little unsettling.

"That's just great. Always loved The Sunshine State!" He passed Jove, approaching Kaine and the door. "Sexy women and phenomenal weed."

Jove fell in a step behind him, trying to find a safe distance that wouldn't alarm them.

"Hey, camera man," Charles gave Kaine's shoulder a companionable slap. "Grab granny and follow me."

Kaine complied, bending over his grandmother's still form and lifting her over his shoulder. He was a strong kid, and she was small.

Good.

Charles stepped up to the door, and Jove watched the hand with the doorknob, the relic, he was sure of it. A metal peg, not quite a spike, jutted from the back end of the relic, and Jove saw where it slotted into the brass key plate on the closed door.

Jove moved a step closer, and when Kaine almost bumped into him on his way to Charles, moved a step closer still to avoid the collision.

Charles lined the doorknob's peg up with the key

plate's slot, and as if drawn into place by magnetism, the relic slid from his hand and fixed itself onto the door.

Kaine stopped behind Charles, patient and unmoving as a machine.

Charles gripped the knob and turned it. A faint hum and crackle, like static electricity, came from the narrow space between door and frame as he opened it, then faded to nothing.

Charles swung the door wide, and Jove saw what looked like the inside of a storage unit or cargo truck box. He stepped aside and motioned Kaine through.

Jove couldn't help a quick glance back over his shoulder. His father sat at the desk, powering up the laptop computer, plugging in a wireless router.

Wow, they have Internet here, Jove thought. Somehow that seemed to be the strangest feature of this strange day.

An Internet connection to another world.

The air in the doorway seemed almost solid as Kaine passed through it, like a sheet of standing water or a frozen smoke. It parted around him, then closed behind.

He shivered violently as he stopped on the other side.

Charles stepped in front of the door to follow him through.

This was it. He'd have to be quick. Very quick.

"Hey, Uncle Chuck!"

Charles paused before stepping through and turned.

Jove crouched and leapt, pumping his wings twice to carry him across the distance between them. He landed at Charles's feet, and when the strange man was finished turning, Jove took him by the shoulders and put his face, beak to nose, to Charles's.

Their eyes met, and when Charles tried to turn his away Jove moved his head to hold the gaze.

If Charles blinked or closed his eyes now the plan would fail.

Charles did not blink. He did not close his eyes. He seemed frozen in place, and as Jove watched, his Uncle Chuck's eyes went solid black and grew even wider. He'd seen the reflection of his own eyes in Jove's, and had become trapped in it.

"Jove, no!" His father's voice, alarmed, angry.

Jove shoved Charles aside and gripped the doorknob. It buzzed briefly in his hand, grew warm as what ever magic it held licked out to taste him. He braced a foot against the door, and pulled.

At first the knob held fast. Jove twisted and strained, then felt the grind of metal against metal as the peg slid from the key plate.

There was a crash behind him as his father's desk tipped over and hit the stone floor. "What the hell are you doing?"

Even as his father spoke, Jove heard his wings swish open and beat at the air.

The doorknob pulled free from its door, and Jove almost tumbled over backward. The door, his foot still braced against it, began to swing shut.

Jove tottered for a second longer, then fell backward. Instead of hitting the floor, he fell against the tall body of his father, the monster. A clawed hand fell on his shoulder.

The door was only inches from closing.

"What the fuck am I doing down here?" Charles shouted from the floor, his voice at once shocked and amused, like a drunk who has awakened in the ball pit of his local McDonalds.

Another clawed hand clamped around his left forearm as he reached for the door.

I'm screwed, Jove thought.

But before the door closed, the tip of his left wing swept forward and wedged itself in the remaining inch-wide crack between this world and the other. With a cry of satisfaction, he threw the door wide open.

The barrier inside the open door grew hazier by the moment, thicker, less translucent. He could see Kaine standing inside the back of the van, his grandmother still in his arms. Waiting for Charles to follow him through.

If I ever see him again, I'm going to punch him right in the face, Jove thought.

But maybe by then, if that day ever came, he'd just give it a pass. Turn the other cheek, as Father Simon would have encouraged him to do.

Because of Kaine's meddling, he was with his real father now, and Uncle Chuck. Between the three of them, they might make a half-functional family.

If, that was, he could break them of their unfortunate habit of kidnapping people.

Jove threw the relic clutched in his right hand through the fading barrier between the worlds, and bracing himself against his father's embrace, kicked the door shut.

Maybe for good.

It closed with a bang that echoed through the wide chamber, and stayed closed.

His father's grip on his right shoulder and left arm tightened, then relaxed.

"*Why?*" The high, reedy voice seemed strained with anger. "Why did you do that?"

Jove pulled himself free of his father's slack grip and turned to face him. The anger in Andy Crow's voice, real or imagined, was not reflected in his posture. He was slumped forward, his wings drooping against the floor, rubbing his head with one hand.

"I thought you'd figure that out on your own," Jove said. "I just wanted to be a hero one more time."

Ten seconds of dead silence followed these words, then Charles broke it in his usual fashion.

"You little scamp!" A shout, but not of anger. Shock and incredulity. "My smoke was on the other side of that fucking door."

To Jove's surprise, Andy Crow began to bellow laughter.

Kaine Moran was aware of waiting, waiting for what seemed to be a long time, but was aware of nothing else.

The thing he waited for never came.

The sun did, a weak glow filtering through the windshield of the van, through the opening from the cab to the mostly empty cargo box. A weak glow at first, then strengthening until bright light that shone down on all possible versions of this third stone from the star Sol hit him in the face and made him blink.

Then he became aware of his dry, burning eyes, and the leaden pain in his arms.

His Grandma Vicky was in them, the sun shining on her face, her squinted eyes. "Kaine, what's going on?"

A good question, and one he didn't have any solid answers to. But he had a suspicion.

"I think we finally found The Puget Devil," Kaine said. "Or maybe he found us."

"Well to hell with that!" She struggled in his arms, and he set her gently on her feet, the aching in his arms eased a bit, but they still throbbed. "If this is how he treats his admirers then to hell with him too!"

"No more Puget Devil," Kaine agreed.

The last few weeks of his life had stretched his personal weirdness boundaries, and the near perfect mental blankness of the past ... how ever long ... had pushed through them.

No more weird tabloid shit.

"Come on, lets get out of this box and go home."

Kaine gave the free-standing door one last sidelong glance before following his Grandma Vicky into the passthrough between the cargo box and cab. He didn't notice the door-knob, twin to the one in the out of place door, on the floor by the roll-up cargo door.

Home, as it turned out, wasn't far away.

They emerged from the van into a twenty-four-hour parking garage and called a cab from the first phone booth they found outside.

Kaine leaned against the booth, exhausted, confused, trying to make sense of the few scattered images he could pull from his mistreated memories of the past few days. His Grandma Vicky leaned against him, her eyes closed.

"I'm going to sleep the rest of the day, and first thing tomorrow morning I'm getting a Venti Caramel Macchiato."

Kaine smiled.

His first priority, after a day or two of uninterrupted sleep, was a new camera. He couldn't remember where his old one was, but did know it was gone.

He wanted to get back to doing what he liked best, painting and photography, but with a definite change in the subject matter.

No more monsters.

So, what then? More Seattle cityscapes? Those were so …

"Passé," he whispered.

What then?

Cactuses, of course. What else was there?

AFTERWORD

The Wrong Side of the Door

My favorite thing about They Call Us Monsters was writing Charles Greene's part in it. I knew both Andy Crow and Charles Greene would play much bigger roles in this story, but I honestly expected Crow to be the breakaway character of They Call Us Monsters, and for Greene to repeat the supporting role he played in 1200 AM Live.

Mr. Greene was having none of it.

I also didn't expect them to be as roguish and likable as they turned out to be. Remember the mean shit they pulled in 1200 Am Live, or the way they met and *acquired* the woman who would eventually give birth to Jove?

Andy Crow said it himself.

We are not the good guys, and we never will be.

Still, I found myself cheering them on, and mostly because of Mr. Greene. He's as likable of bad guy as I've ever written, and even though this story is over, I don't think I'm finished with him yet. As for Crow and Jove, I don't know.

What I do know is that all three of them are now stuck on the wrong side of a door they can't open again. I know that Jove was determined to remain a hero, even if his last heroic act was to lock himself, his monstrous father, and their deranged sidekick out of our world forever. I know that Crow is a bounty hunter, and I bet there is enough work in his own world to keep him busy.

I know that Crow and Greene, maybe especially Greene, are crafty. I know they've found their way into our world once, and I know that the relic doorknobs that opened their way between alternate Earths aren't the only way to travel between the worlds.

I suspect that Crow might be content to kick around his own world for a while, might try to make up for lost time with his son, might even moderate his behavior a bit to encourage Jove to join the family business.

I suspect that Charles Greene may not be content to stay on his side of that closed door for long. I suspect there was a reason he chose to hang out with his friend Andy in a place where humans are the real monsters. Remember, his own people sentenced him to the worst possible death, and as persuasive as he can be, he also tends to piss people off.

Could be there's a bounty out on *him*. Could be he's a bit more motivated to get back to our side of the probability spectrum than his old friend, or the little scamp who stranded them on the wrong side of the door.

I'm almost certain that Charles Greene will be back one of these days, and with any luck I'll get to tell you all about it.

Brian Knight

ABOUT BRIAN KNIGHT

Brian Knight lives in Washington State with his wife and the voices in his head. He has published over a dozen novels, novellas, and collections in the horror, fantasy, and crime genres.

Subscribe to Brian Knight's Knightmares newsletter for news, updates, and free fiction at www.brian-knight.com.